Rise to Lead

A Guide to Unleashing Your Inner Hero and Stop
Being Taken Advantage Of

Paul Sam

KnowHowLeaf Publishing

CONTENTS

Introduction   IV

1. Embracing Your True Potential   1

2. The Psychology of Leadership   14

3. Breaking Free from Limitations   27

4. Communication and Influence   42

5. Decision-Making and Responsibility   57

6. Building Resilience   72

7. Leading with Integrity   84

8. Creating a Vision for Success   98

9. Empowering Others   113

10. Continuous Growth and Development   127

Your Feedback is Important!   139

About the Author   140

Also by Paul Sam   142

INTRODUCTION

Have you ever experienced a situation where you felt undervalued, overlooked, or even exploited? It may happen in a meeting when others are recognized for minimal effort, overlooking your contributions. It may be in your personal life, where your needs frequently take a backseat. While often frustrating and disheartening, these events can serve as powerful catalysts for change. Your inner hero inspires you to embrace challenges, illuminate your path, and lead with confidence and integrity.

The journey toward self-empowerment and authentic leadership is increasingly vital in a fast-paced and competitive society. It's about unlocking the potential that exists within you—a potential that, once realized, can transform both your personal and professional life—not merely about climbing the corporate ladder or achieving personal success. Your roadmap to transformation is "Rise to Lead: A Guide to Unleashing Your Inner Hero and Stop Being Taken Advantage Of."

Envision a world where you confidently recognize your worth and freely share your thoughts. Your leadership combines strength with empathy and resilience, motivating those around you to take action. This journey is achievable, beginning with an understanding and acceptance of your true potential, rather than merely a dream. This book provides the skills and insights necessary to transform your narrative, exploring the depths of your unique abilities while mastering the art of influence and decision-making.

This message is of utmost importance. In the current fast-paced environment, numerous individuals, trapped in a cycle of self-doubt and societal expectations, frequently experience stagnation. The ability to lead becomes increasingly essential when the lines between personal and professional life begin to blur. This book highlights the importance of effective leadership and provides practical techniques to attain it. Examples from real life, practical advice, and inspiring stories can assist you in overcoming challenges while also revealing opportunities for growth and empowerment.

This book offers a comprehensive guide organized into three primary sections. In Part I, "Understanding Your Inner Hero," you will embark on a journey of self-discovery, learning to identify and embrace your unique strengths while overcoming the challenges that lie ahead. This exploration will focus on the psychology of leadership, highlighting the roles of self-awareness and emotional intelligence in shaping effective leaders.

Part II, "Developing Leadership Skills," outlines the essential abilities necessary for effective leadership. The purpose of these chapters is to develop your confidence and effectiveness as a leader by cultivating resilience, enhancing decision-making skills, and refining your communication and influence abilities. You will cultivate your vision, inspire others, and navigate the complexities of leadership with integrity and accountability.

Part III, "Applying Your Skills," focuses on the practical application of the skills you have developed. You will learn how to lead with integrity, create a compelling vision for success, and empower individuals to achieve their fullest potential. This section highlights the significance of mentoring and fostering an empowering culture to ensure that your leadership journey enhances not only your own growth but also that of those around you.

The book offers a narrative that is both educational and deeply engaging from start to finish. The shared stories and case studies aim to resonate with your experiences, challenges, and goals. This book speaks directly to your needs and desires, employing a friendly and empathetic tone that offers companionship and understanding as you embark on your transformative journey.

The journey to discovering your inner hero and embracing your role as a leader is marked by various challenges. Every challenge, however, offers an opportunity for growth in strength, wisdom, and resilience. This book provides a unique blend of storytelling and practical insights that distinguishes it from other self-help and leadership titles, serving as your guide, mentor, and source of inspiration. It offers a unique and valuable approach by bridging the divide between leadership strategies and personal freedom.

Remember that you are not alone as you turn the page and begin this journey. You belong to a growing community of individuals who challenge external definitions and circumstances. United, we will take the initiative to lead both in action and in spirit, transforming our lives and positively impacting those we encounter.

Begin your path to authentic leadership and empowerment today with **_Rise to Lead;_** A manual for realizing your inner hero and avoiding abuse.

Chapter 1

EMBRACING YOUR TRUE POTENTIAL
THE POWER WITHIN YOU

I want you to imagine yourself at the brink of a cliff, gazing out over an expansive and open landscape. The wind blows softly, the horizon extends infinitely ahead, and below, the world presents a mix of fear and endless opportunities. At this moment, the issue isn't whether you should take the leap—it's about whether you genuinely have faith in your ability to soar.

Life frequently offers us figurative cliffs—decisive moments that challenge our potential. Numerous individuals hesitate, persuaded by the whispers of self-doubt or societal pressures that they do not possess the ability to rise above. Within each of us exists a vast reservoir of strength, creativity, and resilience. When we recognise and embrace this potential, it can propel us to remarkable achievements.

This chapter invites you to explore that potential. We will navigate the pathways of self-doubt, confront the challenges posed by societal pressures, and ultimately gain a clearer insight into the unique strengths that empower you to achieve greatness. The journey ahead may present challenges, yet it holds the potential for transformation, personal growth, and the unveiling of the hero within oneself.

Conquering Self-Doubt: The Quiet Adversary

Self-doubt lingers quietly in the back of your mind, consistently poised to challenge your efforts. It challenges your capabilities, overlooks your accomplishments, and emphasises your shortcomings. Where does this doubt originate, and why does it exert such significant influence over us?

Exploring the Origins of Self-Doubt

Self-doubt often takes root in childhood, arising from experiences that challenge our abilities or undermine our confidence. It could have been a critical comment from a teacher, an unsuccessful effort at trying something new, or a comparison to a more successful sibling or peer. These moments, which may appear trivial initially, can build up into a significant obstacle that prevents us from reaching our true potential.

Additionally, societal messages can intensify this uncertainty. We are frequently exposed to images of perfection—successful entrepreneurs, flawless celebrities, and influencers who appear to have everything in order. This constant pressure establishes an unattainable standard, suggesting that perfection is a prerequisite for our worthiness. The outcome? We start to question our value, our skills, and our capacity to reach our full potential.

The Psychological Effects of Self-Doubt

Self-doubt is not merely a mental obstacle; it can also have physical and emotional manifestations, influencing all areas of our lives. This may result in anxiety, depression, and even physical issues like headaches or chronic fatigue. Self-doubt can hinder our willingness to take risks, follow our passions, or venture beyond our comfort zones. We hesitate, steering clear of opportunities that may foster growth, driven by a fear of failure or rejection.

It is essential to understand that self-doubt is not an intrinsic aspect of our identity; rather, it is a behaviour that we acquire over time. Just as any acquired behaviour can be learnt, it is also possible to unlearn it.

Strategies for Conquering Self-Doubt

1. Recognise Your Strengths: A highly effective method to address self-doubt is by acknowledging your strengths. Develop the practice of recognising your achievements, regardless of their size. Keep a journal to record your daily accomplishments and reflect on the skills or qualities that contributed to those successes. With consistent practice, this approach can assist in reshaping your brain to concentrate on your strengths instead of your perceived weaknesses.

2. Confront negative thoughts: When self-doubt emerges, address it directly. Consider whether this thought is grounded in reality or if it is merely a reflection of your fears. Frequently, you may discover that these doubts lack a basis in reality and are, in fact, amplified fears of failure or feelings of inadequacy. By examining these thoughts, you can start to break their influence over you.

3. Envisioning Success: Visualisation serves as a potent technique employed by athletes, performers, and leaders to improve their performance. Take a few moments each day to envision yourself achieving your goals. Envision the specifics—the visuals, auditory elements, and feelings tied to that achievement. This approach can enhance confidence and diminish the influence of self-doubt.

4. Reach out for Assistance: It's important to seek help from others when needed. Discussing your doubts with a trusted friend, mentor, or therapist can provide valuable perspective and help you formulate strategies to address them. At times, simply listening to another person's confidence in your abilities can serve as the motivation you require to begin believing in yourself.

5. Acting in the Face of Fear: Ultimately, the most effective way to conquer self-doubt is through taking action. Every time you venture beyond your comfort zone and strive towards your goals, you diminish the hold of doubt. Begin with manageable steps, and as you build your confidence, progressively tackle larger challenges. Courage is acting despite fear, not the absence of it.

Breaking Free from Societal Pressures—The Invisible Chains

Society exerts a significant influence. It moulds our values, affects our choices, and frequently determines what is viewed as "normal" or "acceptable." What occurs when societal expectations conflict with our authentic selves? How can we manage the pressures to conform while remaining authentic to our individual potential?

The Burden of Expectations

From a young age, we learn to conform to established expectations. Boys are often anticipated to exhibit strength and assertiveness, while girls are expected to embody nurturing and demure qualities. As we develop, these gender roles evolve into wider societal expectations—secure a stable job, marry, have children, purchase a home, and so forth. Although these goals are not inherently problematic, the pressure to attain them can become excessive, particularly if they do not resonate with our genuine aspirations.

Society imposes expectations influenced by race, culture, and socioeconomic status. Individuals from marginalised communities frequently encounter heightened pressures to succeed, aiming to challenge stereotypes or serve as representatives of their community. The expectations placed upon individuals can serve as both a source of motivation and a burden, creating a persistent tension between meeting societal roles and chasing personal goals.

The Implications of Conformity

Conforming to societal pressures can lead to acceptance, yet it often results in a loss of our true selves along the way. We often suppress our true desires, talents, and dreams to meet societal expectations. Over time, this may result in feelings of emptiness, dissatisfaction, and a sense of living a life that does not truly belong to you.

Additionally, conformity hinders innovation and creativity. When everyone adheres to the same course, there is limited opportunity for innovative ideas or diverse viewpoints. Society requires individuals who are bold enough to think outside the box, who question established norms, and who are committed to following their distinct vision, even when faced with resistance.

Approaches to Achieving Liberation

1. Define Your Own Success: To liberate yourself from societal expectations, the first step is to determine what success means to you. This necessitates self-reflection and sincerity. Consider this: What are my genuine passions? What type of life do I aspire to live? Which values hold the greatest significance for me? Defining success on your own terms allows you to craft a life that resonates with your authentic self, rather than conforming to external expectations.

2. Establish Boundaries: It is essential to establish boundaries with individuals who impose their expectations on you, whether they are family, friends, or society as a whole. This may involve declining certain commitments, separating yourself from detrimental influences, or expressing your needs and desires more effectively. It is important to recognise that you have the right to live your life in alignment with your own values and priorities.

3. Surround Yourself with Supportive People: Look for individuals who inspire you to embrace your true self. These could include friends, mentors, or even online communities that align with your values and interests. Being around supportive individuals can strengthen your confidence and offer the motivation necessary to reach your true potential.

4. Practice self-compassion: It can be challenging to break free from societal pressures, and there may be moments when you experience self-doubt or encounter criticism. During these times, it is important to practice self-compassion. Remember that it is perfectly acceptable to make mistakes, face challenges, and embrace imperfections. Extend to yourself the same compassion and empathy that you would readily give to a dear friend.

5. Embrace Authenticity: Ultimately, aim to embody authenticity in your daily life. This involves being authentic in your thoughts, words, and actions. Making difficult choices may be necessary, but the reward is a life that truly belongs to you—one that embodies your unique potential and aspirations.

Techniques for Self-Discovery: A Journey to Understanding Yourself

Self-discovery involves revealing your authentic self, including your strengths, weaknesses, passions, and values. It involves uncovering the layers of conditioning and expectations to expose your true self. This journey is vital for those looking to realise their true potential, offering the clarity and insight necessary for making informed and intentional decisions.

The Importance of self-discovery

Without self-discovery, we resemble ships lost at sea, navigating wherever the currents lead us. While we can reach specific goals or attain various statuses, lacking a profound understanding of ourselves can render these accomplishments feeling empty or unsatisfying. Self-discovery serves as the guiding compass that leads us to a life filled with meaning and purpose.

Additionally, self-discovery enables us to recognise and utilise our distinct strengths. Each individual possesses a unique blend of skills, talents, and experiences that distinguishes them from others. By gaining insight into these aspects, we can concentrate on the areas where we are most likely to achieve success and experience fulfilment.

Methods for Personal Exploration

1. Journaling: Writing serves as an effective means for self-exploration. This approach enables you to thoughtfully examine your thoughts, emotions, and experiences in an organised manner. Begin by allocating time each day to document your goals, fears, desires, and reflections. As time progresses, patterns will become apparent, offering a deeper understanding of your authentic self. Journaling can aid in clarifying your thoughts and facilitating decision-making that aligns with your values.

2. Personality Assessments: Instruments such as the Myers-Briggs Type Indicator (MBTI), StrengthsFinder, or the Enneagram offer valuable insights into your personality, strengths, and preferences. Although no assessment can completely encompass the intricacies of your identity, these tools can provide a foundation for further exploration.

3. Mindfulness and Meditation: Engaging in mindfulness practices can enhance your awareness of thoughts, emotions, and physical sensations. This increased awareness can foster deeper self-understanding and assist you in recognising aspects of your life that require attention or transformation. Meditation can calm the mind and foster introspection, enabling a connection with your deeper self.

4. Seek Feedback: Occasionally, others may notice aspects about us that we might overlook ourselves. Gathering feedback from reliable friends, family, or colleagues can offer important perspectives on your strengths and opportunities for improvement. Embrace constructive criticism while ensuring you evaluate feedback in light of your personal values and objectives.

5. Explore New Experiences: A great way to uncover your true potential is to step outside your comfort zone and embrace new opportunities. Engaging in new experiences, whether it involves acquiring a new skill, exploring a different location, or embracing a fresh challenge, can uncover latent talents and passions. They assist in developing confidence and resilience, both of which are crucial for personal growth.

The Advantages of Self-Discovery

Self-discovery offers significant advantages. By gaining a deeper understanding of yourself, you will be more capable of making decisions that reflect your true desires. Your pursuits will bring you greater fulfilment, as they will be driven by a sense of purpose rather than by external expectations.

Self-discovery promotes self-acceptance. Embracing your strengths while recognising your weaknesses allows you to foster inner peace and confidence. This enables you to pursue your goals with enhanced determination and resilience.

Building Confidence—The Cornerstone of Success

Confidence is the assurance in your capacity to achieve success. It serves as the basis for all accomplishments. Lacking confidence, even the most skilled individuals may struggle, hindered by fear and self-doubt. Confidence is not a fixed trait; it can be cultivated and enhanced gradually.

The Role of Confidence in Success

Confidence is essential for achieving success. Your approach to challenges, interactions with others, and self-perception are all influenced by this. Individuals with confidence tend to embrace risks, pursue their objectives with resolve, and persist when confronted with challenges. They are also more likely to instill confidence in others, potentially resulting in increased opportunities and support.

Confidence also influences your mental and emotional well-being. Having confidence in yourself makes you more resilient against negative opinions and setbacks. Maintaining a positive outlook, even in challenging situations, is crucial for achieving long-term success.

Methods for Enhancing Self-Confidence

1. Establish and accomplish small goals: A highly effective method for building confidence is to establish and accomplish small, manageable goals. Every time you achieve a goal, regardless of its size, you strengthen your confidence in your capabilities. As your confidence increases, you can progressively establish larger goals, leveraging your achievements.

2. Develop Competence: Confidence is closely associated with competence; the greater your skills in a specific area, the more confident you will become. Invest time in enhancing your skills and knowledge in areas that matter to you. This may include enrolling in courses, engaging in regular practice, or pursuing mentorship opportunities. As your skills develop, your confidence will also grow.

3. Embrace Failure as a Learning Opportunity: Failure is an inherent aspect of the learning journey, yet it can significantly impact your confidence if not approached with the appropriate mindset. Rather than perceiving failure as a measure of your capabilities, consider it a chance to learn and develop. Evaluate the issues that occurred, implement necessary changes, and make another attempt. As time goes on, this resilience will enhance your confidence.

4. Engage in Positive Self-Talk: The manner in which you communicate with yourself greatly influences your confidence. Constantly criticising yourself or dwelling on your shortcomings can undermine your confidence. Focus on engaging in positive self-talk. Recognise your strengths, take pride in your accomplishments, and reflect on your previous successes. This change in perspective can significantly enhance your confidence.

5. Surround Yourself with Positive Influences: The individuals in your life can significantly impact your confidence, either enhancing it or diminishing it. Find people who support your aspirations and motivate you to achieve your objectives. Steer clear of individuals who are excessively critical or negative, as they may diminish your confidence and self-esteem.

The Long-Term Benefits of Confidence

As you develop your confidence, you will observe a change in your approach to life. Challenges that once appeared insurmountable will transform into opportunities for growth. You will embrace greater risks, chase your goals with increased resolve, and bounce back more swiftly from challenges. Confidence strengthens your relationships, as people are attracted to your positive energy and self-assurance.

Ultimately, confidence serves as the essential element in realising your true potential. This enables you to transcend fear and self-doubt, empowering you to reach your goals and lead a life filled with purpose and fulfilment.

Conclusion: Embracing Your Inner Hero

As we wrap up this chapter, it is essential to acknowledge that the path to realising your true potential is a continuous journey. It necessitates ongoing self-reflection, bravery, and a dedication to personal development. The rewards are significant—a life that truly reflects who you are, enriched with purpose, fulfilment, and the acknowledgement of your distinct strengths.

Keep in mind that you are the protagonist in your own narrative. The obstacles you encounter, the uncertainties you navigate, and the pressures you withstand are integral to your journey. Embrace these experiences, learn from them, and let them guide you in becoming the person you are destined to be.

Take action today—whether it involves confronting a doubt, establishing a new goal, or merely recognising your strengths. Every step you take brings you nearer to discovering your true potential and awakening the hero within.

Worksheet: Uncovering Your Authentic Potential

Here is a straightforward worksheet intended to assist you in your journey of self-discovery and building confidence.

1. Identify Your Strengths: Spend a few moments noting your five key strengths. These may include skills, personality traits, or areas of knowledge. For each strength, please provide a recent example of how you have applied it.

2. Identify Your Goals: What are your three primary personal or professional objectives? For every goal, outline the necessary steps to accomplish it and recognise any possible challenges you may encounter.

3. Challenge a Doubt: Identify one aspect of your life where you encounter self-doubt. Now, create a positive affirmation that addresses and dispels this doubt. For the upcoming week, please recite this affirmation each day.

4. Consider societal pressure: Identify a societal expectation that has influenced your choices. Consider how this pressure has influenced your life and whether it aligns with your genuine goals.

5. Take a confidence-building action: Choose one small step you can take today to enhance your confidence. This may involve establishing a new objective, acquiring a new skill, or just venturing beyond your comfort zone.

Action Points

- **Recognise Your Strengths:** Develop a daily practice of acknowledging your accomplishments and personal strengths.

- **Confront Self-Doubt:** Examine negative thoughts and substitute them with positive affirmations.

- **Live Authentically:** Establish your own definition of success and chase goals that resonate with your genuine aspirations.

- **Build Confidence:** Enhance your confidence by establishing small, attainable goals and viewing failure as a valuable learning experience.

- **Seek Support:** Surround yourself with positive influences and seek feedback from trusted individuals.

Final Reflection: Becoming the Hero of Your Story

Consider taking a moment to reflect on the insights you've gained from this chapter. What ways can you incorporate these insights into your daily life? What actions will you pursue to fully realise your true potential? Keep in mind that the path to greatness starts with a single step—take that step today and begin living the life you are destined to lead.

Chapter 2

THE PSYCHOLOGY OF LEADERSHIP

THE ESSENCE OF LEADERSHIP

L eadership is frequently viewed as a role characterized by *power, authority, and control.*

True leadership extends beyond mere titles or positions; it represents a significant psychological phenomenon that shapes how you engage, motivate, and foster collaborative efforts.

This chapter explores the complex psychology of leadership, examining the mental and emotional factors that contribute to effective leadership. Grasping these psychological elements enables leaders to effectively manage the intricacies of their positions while allowing them to lead with genuine authenticity, emotional intelligence, and a deep comprehension of human behavior.

In the examination of the psychology of leadership, it is important to understand that leadership does not conform to a universal standard. Various circumstances require distinct leadership approaches, and the capacity to adjust is a defining characteristic of an exceptional leader. Furthermore, emotional intelligence is essential for effective leadership, enabling leaders to engage with their teams more profoundly, build trust, and promote a positive workplace atmosphere.

In this chapter, we will explore different leadership styles, analyzing their psychological underpinnings, advantages, and possible drawbacks. We will examine the importance of emotional intelligence in leadership, providing insights into how leaders can utilize this powerful asset to lead with authenticity and effectiveness. Upon completing this chapter, you will have a more profound insight into the psychological foundations of leadership, providing you with the knowledge and skills necessary to become the leader you aim to be.

Understanding Leadership Approaches: The Psychological Foundations

The Autocratic Leader: Authority and Direction

The autocratic leadership style is marked by a command-and-control approach, originating from traditional hierarchical structures in which the leader possesses absolute authority. This approach is grounded in a psychological desire for control and order, with the leader holding the belief that their vision is essential and should be implemented without deviation.

From a psychological standpoint, autocratic leaders often display characteristics linked to a strong desire for power and control. They are frequently motivated by a need to oversee every facet of the organization or team, making certain that their instructions are adhered to precisely. This leadership approach can prove beneficial in scenarios that demand swift decision-making, particularly in crisis management or military operations.

Nonetheless, it can hinder creativity and innovation, as team members might feel disempowered and hesitant to share their ideas.

Although autocratic leadership may prove effective in specific situations, it frequently results in diminished trust and morale among team members. Team members may experience feelings of resentment, frustration, and disengagement when they are not given the opportunity to participate in the decision-making process. Over time, this may lead to elevated turnover rates and an unhealthy work environment.

The Democratic Leader: Collaboration and Consensus

Unlike the autocratic style, democratic leadership is based on the principles of collaboration and collective decision-making. Democratic leaders value collaboration and are dedicated to engaging their team members in the decision-making process. This approach to leadership is based on the psychological principles of fairness, equality, and mutual respect.

Democratic leaders demonstrate significant emotional intelligence, especially regarding empathy and social awareness. They possess the ability to understand the emotions and needs of their team members, fostering an environment where everyone feels appreciated and listened to. This approach encourages team members to take ownership and responsibility, as they play an active role in influencing the direction of the organization or project.

From a psychological perspective, democratic leadership may result in increased job satisfaction and engagement. When team members have a voice in the decision-making process, they are more likely to feel motivated and committed to the organization's goals. Nonetheless, this leadership approach can be time-intensive, as achieving consensus frequently necessitates thorough discussion and negotiation. In circumstances that require prompt decision-making, democratic leadership might not be the most efficient strategy.

The Transformational Leader: Inspiring Change

Transformational leadership is a style that is fundamentally based on the principles of inspiration and motivation. Transformational leaders are visionaries who aim to inspire and uplift their team members, motivating them to surpass their perceived limitations and attain remarkable outcomes. This leadership style emphasizes personal and organizational growth, with the leader serving as a catalyst for change.

Transformational leaders demonstrate a strong level of emotional intelligence, especially regarding self-awareness and self-regulation. They excel at regulating their emotions and actions, enabling them to stay calm and composed when confronted with challenges. Transformational leaders excel at inspiring and motivating others, frequently utilizing compelling narratives and a clear vision for the future.

Transformational leadership can bring about significant changes within an organization, as team members are inspired to rise above their individual interests for the collective benefit. This approach to leadership promotes an environment where innovation and creativity thrive, empowering team members to think creatively and question existing norms. Nonetheless, a strong emphasis on change and growth may occasionally result in burnout, especially when leaders set unrealistic expectations or when team members feel inundated by the demands they face.

The Servant Leader: Prioritizing the Needs of Others

Servant leadership is a style grounded in the principles of altruism and service. Servant leaders focus on the needs of their team members, placing them above their own, and strive to empower and support others in reaching their full potential. This leadership approach is defined by a strong dedication to the welfare and growth of those they guide.

Servant leaders demonstrate psychological traits that reflect strong empathy, compassion, and humility. They are motivated by a commitment to assist others and to foster a positive and supportive workplace atmosphere. Servant leaders are frequently regarded as mentors and coaches, steering their team members towards both personal and professional development.

Servant leadership fosters elevated levels of trust, loyalty, and job satisfaction within teams. When individuals sense that their leader truly values their well-being and success, they are more inclined to be engaged and dedicated to the organization's objectives. Servant leadership presents its own set of challenges, as the leader is required to find a balance between the needs of the team and the demands of the organization. This leadership style might be less effective in scenarios that demand strong and decisive leadership.

The Laissez-Faire Leader: Freedom and Autonomy

Laissez-faire leadership is a style grounded in the principles of autonomy and independence. Laissez-faire leaders adopt a hands-off approach, empowering their team members to make decisions and manage their own work with minimal supervision. This leadership style emphasizes a strong trust in the capabilities of the team and values the significance of individual autonomy.

From a psychological perspective, laissez-faire leaders demonstrate characteristics linked to a low desire for control and a strong belief in their team's abilities. They hold the view that individuals are naturally driven and able to oversee their own tasks without requiring ongoing oversight. This method can be especially beneficial in settings where team members possess strong skills and are driven to succeed independently.

Laissez-faire leadership encourages empowerment and creativity within teams by allowing members the freedom to explore new ideas and approaches. However, when team members lack self-discipline or establish unclear goals and expectations, this leadership approach may lead to a lack of direction and accountability. In certain situations, laissez-faire leadership may lead to a disorganized work environment where tasks remain unfinished and deadlines are overlooked.

The Role of Emotional Intelligence in Leadership

Understanding Emotional Intelligence

Emotional intelligence (EI) plays a vital role in successful leadership. Emotional intelligence fundamentally involves the capacity to identify, comprehend, and regulate both personal emotions and those of others. Emotional intelligence plays a crucial role in leadership, allowing leaders to effectively manage intricate interpersonal relationships, foster strong connections, and cultivate a positive workplace atmosphere.

Emotional intelligence consists of four essential components:

1. Self-awareness: The capacity to identify and comprehend one's own emotions, strengths, weaknesses, and values. Self-awareness enables leaders to stay grounded and genuine in their interactions with others.

2. Self-regulation: The capacity to control one's emotions and actions in alignment with personal values and objectives. Self-regulation allows leaders to maintain their composure and calmness, even when faced with stress or challenges.

3. Social Awareness: The capacity to comprehend and relate to the feelings and viewpoints of others. Social awareness enables leaders to foster strong relationships and cultivate a supportive and inclusive workplace.

4. Relationship Management: The capacity to influence, inspire, and lead others toward a positive outcome. Managing relationships requires clear communication, the skill to resolve conflicts, and the capacity to motivate and inspire those around you.

The Influence of Emotional Intelligence on Leadership

Leaders who possess strong emotional intelligence tend to excel in their positions, as they are more adept at navigating the emotional intricacies of leadership. Emotional intelligence enables leaders to establish trust, encourage collaboration, and cultivate a positive and inclusive workplace atmosphere. Furthermore, leaders with emotional intelligence tend to inspire and motivate their teams, resulting in increased engagement and productivity.

A significant advantage of emotional intelligence in leadership is the capacity to foster strong and trusting relationships. When leaders are aware of the emotions and needs of their team members, they can more effectively offer the support and guidance essential for success. This fosters an environment of psychological safety within the team, allowing individuals to feel valued, respected, and empowered to deliver their best work.

Emotional intelligence is essential in resolving conflicts effectively. Leaders who possess strong emotional intelligence excel at managing interpersonal conflicts and approaching issues in a constructive and solution-oriented manner. This prevents the escalation of conflicts and guarantees a fair and equitable resolution for all parties involved.

Additionally, emotional intelligence allows leaders to effectively handle stress and maintain resilience when confronted with challenges. Leaders who understand and manage their own emotions can remain calm and composed, even in challenging situations. This approach not only enables the leader to maintain focus and effectiveness but also offers the team a sense of stability and reassurance.

Enhancing Emotional Intelligence in Leadership

Although certain individuals may inherently have a strong level of emotional intelligence, it is also a skill that can be cultivated and enhanced over time. Leaders can employ various strategies to improve their emotional intelligence.

1. Engage in self-reflection: Consistently set aside time to consider your emotions, thoughts, and actions. Reflect on how your emotions influence your decisions and interactions with others. This practice can enhance your self-awareness and self-regulation skills.

2. Request Feedback: Solicit input from reliable colleagues, mentors, or team members. Gaining insights into how others view your emotional intelligence can be beneficial and can assist you in pinpointing areas that may need enhancement.

3. Cultivate Empathy: Actively strive to comprehend and connect with the feelings and viewpoints of those around you. Engaging in active listening, asking questions for deeper insight, and reflecting on the effects of your actions on others are essential components of this process.

4. Improve Communication Skills: Effective communication is an essential aspect of emotional intelligence. Engage in active listening, maintain clear and open communication, and develop the ability to express your emotions constructively and respectfully.

5. Manage Stress: Create effective strategies to handle stress and sustain emotional equilibrium. This may encompass mindfulness practices, physical activity, and effective coping strategies.

Leaders can improve their capacity to lead effectively and authentically by cultivating emotional intelligence. This approach helps the leader and improves team performance.

Case Studies: Leadership in Practice

Case Study 1: Nelson Mandela: A Leader of Empathy and Reconciliation

Nelson Mandela is frequently recognized as one of the most influential leaders of the 20th century. His leadership was marked by a profound sense of compassion, forgiveness, and a dedication to justice and equality. Mandela's leadership style was grounded in the principles of servant leadership, emphasizing his commitment to serving the people of South Africa and fostering reconciliation and healing following decades of apartheid.

Mandela's leadership was fundamentally supported by a significant level of emotional intelligence. He exhibited exceptional self-awareness and self-regulation, maintaining calmness and composure despite having spent 27 years in prison. Mandela's capacity to understand the perspectives of both his supporters and his former oppressors enabled him to create connections and promote unity in a nation marked by deep divisions.

One of the most compelling instances of Mandela's emotional intelligence was his choice to forgive those who had imprisoned him and to advocate for reconciliation instead of seeking revenge. This approach not only helped to prevent further bloodshed but also established a strong example of leadership rooted in compassion and humanity.

Case Study 2: Steve Jobs: A Visionary Leader with a Multifaceted Approach

Steve Jobs, co-founder of Apple Inc., was recognized for his visionary leadership and his capacity to inspire and propel innovation. Jobs' leadership style was multifaceted, incorporating aspects of autocratic, transformational, and laissez-faire approaches. Although he was frequently demanding and precise in his expectations, he possessed a remarkable talent for motivating his team to exceed the limits of what could be achieved.

From a psychological perspective, Jobs demonstrated significant self-awareness and self-regulation, especially in his later years. He was recognized for his remarkable focus and capacity to maintain composure in high-pressure situations, enabling him to guide Apple through times of considerable change and innovation.

Nonetheless, Jobs' leadership style was characterized by a deficiency in empathy and social awareness, frequently resulting in conflicts with his team members. Despite this, Jobs successfully fostered an innovative culture at Apple, inspiring his team to develop groundbreaking products that would transform the world.

Jobs' leadership legacy exemplifies the impact of visionary leadership while also highlighting the importance of emotional intelligence in fostering strong and sustainable relationships with others.

Conclusion: Harnessing the Power of Psychology in Leadership

The psychology of leadership is a complex and multifaceted area that includes various emotional, cognitive, and behavioral elements. Grasping these psychological foundations is crucial for anyone looking to lead in a genuine and effective manner.

This chapter examines various leadership styles and their psychological underpinnings, ranging from the command-and-control approach characteristic of autocratic leaders to the collaborative and inclusive methods employed by democratic leaders. We have also explored the essential role of emotional intelligence in leadership, emphasizing how self-awareness, self-regulation, social awareness, and relationship management are fundamental to establishing trust, promoting collaboration, and motivating others.

Ultimately, the most effective leaders are those who can adjust their leadership style to meet the demands of the situation while also demonstrating authenticity and emotional intelligence. Utilizing the principles of psychology in leadership enables you to enhance your effectiveness, compassion, and ability to inspire, ultimately driving positive change and leaving a lasting impact on your team.

Action Points: Applying the Psychology of Leadership

1. Identify Your Leadership Style: Take a moment to reflect on your current leadership style and evaluate how it corresponds with the psychological principles outlined in this chapter. Are there any aspects of your approach that you might consider more flexible or adaptable?

2. Enhance Your Emotional Intelligence: Focus on improving your emotional intelligence through self-reflection, soliciting feedback, and cultivating empathy and communication abilities.

3. Adjust your Leadership approach to the circumstances: Take into account the requirements of your team and the environment in which you are guiding them. Be open to adjusting your leadership approach to suit the circumstances, whether that involves taking a more directive, collaborative, or hands-off stance.

4. Lead with Authenticity: Aim to lead in a manner that reflects your core values and principles. Genuine leadership cultivates trust and respect within your team.

5. Foster Strong Relationships: Dedicate time and effort to cultivate strong, trusting connections with your team members. Fostering a positive work environment will increase your leadership effectiveness.

Summary & Recap

This chapter delves into the psychology of leadership, examining various leadership styles and the importance of emotional intelligence. We explored the psychological underpinnings of autocratic, democratic, transformational, servant, and laissez-faire leadership, emphasizing the advantages and possible challenges associated with each approach. We also talked about the essential role of emotional intelligence in leadership, highlighting the significance of self-awareness, self-regulation, social awareness, and relationship management.

Understanding the psychological foundations of leadership enables you to become a more effective and genuine leader, allowing you to tailor your approach to suit the needs of your team and the specific circumstances you face. Regardless of whether you are at the helm of a small team or a large organization, the insights presented in this chapter will assist you in navigating the complexities of leadership with both confidence and compassion.

Final Reflection: Leadership as a continuous journey

Leadership is a journey characterized by ongoing learning and development. As you contemplate the insights acquired from this chapter, think about how you can implement them in your own leadership journey. What actions can you implement to improve your emotional intelligence, adjust your leadership approach, and lead with genuine authenticity? What strategies can you implement to strengthen relationships within your team and foster a positive and supportive workplace atmosphere?

As you progress in your leadership journey, keep in mind that the most successful leaders are those who embrace learning, growth, and adaptability. Embracing the psychology of leadership allows you to tap into your inner hero, leading with confidence, compassion, and integrity.

Chapter 3

BREAKING FREE FROM LIMITATIONS
THE UNSEEN BONDS

Envision a bird raised in confinement, unaware of the vast skies that lie beyond its enclosure. The bars that surround it serve as both its safeguard and confinement. For this bird, the idea of flying freely is as unfamiliar as walking on water. What would happen if, one day, the cage door were to open? Would the bird risk venturing out or stay in its enclosure, afraid of the unknown?

Similar to this bird, many individuals find themselves confined by self-imposed limitations. These cages are built from individual insecurities, previous failures, societal pressures, and fears—whether they are tangible or not.

This chapter aims to identify these constraints, explore their formation, and ultimately find a way to overcome them. The objective is not merely to overcome our limitations but to rise above them, revealing the inner hero that exists within each of us.

To overcome limitations, we must first recognize that they are present. It is essential to address both the personal and external obstacles that impede our progress, exploring their origins and recognizing their influence on our behaviors and mindset. This chapter will examine these barriers thoroughly and offer strategies to address them effectively. By the end of this chapter, you will have the tools to break free from the constraints that bind you, as well as the confidence to overcome the limitations that have previously held you back.

The Anatomy of Limitations: Personal Barriers

All limitations originate in the mind. The way we think shapes our reality, affecting both our self-perception and our view of the world around us. Personal barriers can be particularly deceptive as they are self-imposed, frequently presenting themselves as truths or beliefs. To overcome these barriers, we must first acknowledge them as constructs of our own creation.

1. Self-Doubt: The Inner Saboteur

Self-doubt is arguably one of the most widespread personal barriers. It's the persistent voice in your mind that doubts your abilities, diminishes your confidence, and leads you to believe that you fall short. The internal saboteur can be debilitating, hindering your ability to pursue opportunities, take risks, or venture beyond your comfort zone.

Where does self-doubt originate? It frequently arises from previous experiences—failures, rejections, or criticisms that have made a significant impression. As time passes, these experiences form a narrative that you start to accept: "I'm not capable," "I'm not smart enough," "I don't deserve success." This narrative creates a self-fulfilling prophecy, restricting your potential and confining you to a cycle of inaction.

To address self-doubt, it is essential to confront this narrative. Begin by acknowledging negative self-talk as a distortion of reality. Substitute it with uplifting affirmations that emphasize your value and abilities. Surround yourself with individuals who support you and foster your development.

Above all, it is essential to take action, even when uncertainty arises. Every step taken, regardless of its size, fosters confidence and diminishes the hold of self-doubt.

2. Fear of Failure: The Perception of Perfection

Fear of failure is a prevalent obstacle that prevents individuals from moving forward. It is the fear of making mistakes, of not meeting standards, of failing to fulfill expectations—whether our own or those imposed by others. This fear can be so overpowering that it hinders our attempts, resulting in a life filled with missed opportunities and unrealized potential.

This fear often arises from a mistaken belief that we must completely avoid failure. We often associate failure with a sense of inadequacy, perceiving it as a reflection of a fundamental flaw in our character. In reality, failure does not define our identity; rather, it is an inherent aspect of the learning journey. Every successful person has faced failure at some point—often on numerous occasions. Their distinguishing feature is the capacity to learn from errors, adapt, and continue progressing.

To address the fear of failure, you must shift your perspective. Rather than perceiving failure as a setback, consider it a chance for development. Take in the lessons it provides and apply them to enhance and polish your approach. Keep in mind that perfection is an illusion; everyone faces setbacks on their journey to success. The essential aspect is not to evade failure but to gain insights from it and continue progressing.

3. Impostor Syndrome: A Veil of Insufficiency

Impostor syndrome refers to a psychological phenomenon where individuals question their achievements and harbor fears of being revealed as a *"fraud."* Even with clear evidence of their abilities, individuals facing impostor syndrome often feel unworthy of their achievements and think they have somehow deceived others into believing they are more skilled than they truly are.

This syndrome is especially prevalent among high achievers, who establish extremely high standards for themselves and frequently measure their accomplishments against those of others. The outcome is a widespread feeling of inadequacy, even in the face of clear evidence to the contrary.

Addressing impostor syndrome necessitates a change in viewpoint. Begin by acknowledging that feelings of inadequacy are a common aspect of the human experience. At some point, everyone experiences doubts about their abilities, particularly when confronted with new challenges. Rather than allowing these doubts to overwhelm you, recognize them and continue to progress regardless. Take a moment to reflect on your achievements and the dedication that contributed to reaching them. Request input from reliable colleagues or mentors who can offer an unbiased view of your skills. Above all, refrain from comparing yourself to others. Concentrate on your personal journey and the advancements you have achieved instead of comparing yourself to outside standards.

4. Limiting Beliefs: The Narratives We Create

Limiting beliefs are firmly established convictions that we possess regarding ourselves, others, or the surrounding world. Early experiences, cultural influences, or societal norms frequently give rise to beliefs, which significantly shape our perception of achievable goals. For instance, you may think, *"I'm too old to begin a new career," "I'll never achieve financial success,"* or *"I'm not creative enough to follow my passion."*

These beliefs act as unseen restraints that bind us to a restricted understanding of who we can be. Self-imposed boundaries can hinder our ability to explore new opportunities and reach our full potential.

Identifying the limiting beliefs that are holding you back is the first step in breaking free from these chains.

After identifying these beliefs, it is important to challenge them. Consider whether this belief is genuinely accurate. Where did it originate? Is it beneficial to me, or is it hindering my progress? Frequently, you may discover that these beliefs stem from outdated assumptions or baseless fears. By examining and reinterpreting these beliefs, you can start to break down the obstacles they impose.

5. Perfectionism: The Quest for an Unattainable Standard

Perfectionism is the unwavering quest for excellence. Striving for excellence is admirable, but perfectionism can lead to an unhealthy level of expectation. Perfectionists establish exceedingly high expectations for themselves and those around them, which can frequently result in ongoing stress, burnout, and a sense of dissatisfaction. They are apprehensive about making mistakes or not meeting expectations, which can hinder their ability to take action or finish tasks.

The irony of perfectionism is that it frequently results in the very outcomes it aims to prevent. The anxiety surrounding the pursuit of perfection can lead to procrastination, as individuals who strive for perfection may postpone initiating or finishing tasks to evade the chance of failing. When they take action, they frequently become overly critical of their results, resulting in a cycle of self-blame and frustration.

To address perfectionism, it is essential to accept imperfection. Recognize that errors are an inherent aspect of learning and that perfection is unattainable for anyone. Establish achievable objectives and prioritize advancement over flawless outcomes. Embrace self-compassion and acknowledge your worth and capabilities, irrespective of the pursuit of perfection. Releasing the desire for perfection allows you to embrace risks, explore new opportunities, and ultimately attain greater success.

The External Barriers: Societal and Environmental Limitations

Personal barriers are internal, whereas external barriers are influenced by the surrounding environment. Barriers such as societal expectations, cultural norms, economic constraints, and various external factors can restrict our opportunities and influence our behavior. Recognizing and addressing these obstacles is crucial for liberating ourselves from constraints and realizing our complete potential.

1. Societal Expectations: The Burden of Conformity

Society establishes a range of expectations for individuals influenced by their gender, race, socioeconomic status, and various other factors. These expectations often define what is considered "acceptable" or "normal" behavior, which can be constraining. For example, society may expect women to prioritize caregiving responsibilities over their professional aspirations, while the culture may encourage men to conceal their emotions and prioritize financial achievement.

Societal expectations can impose considerable pressure to conform, causing individuals to hide their authentic selves and ambitions in order to blend in. This may lead to a diminished sense of identity, feelings of unfulfillment, and the continuation of restrictive beliefs.

To liberate yourself from societal expectations, it is essential to first acknowledge how they shape your behavior. Take a moment to think about the expectations placed upon you and evaluate if they resonate with your personal values and aspirations. Defy these expectations by celebrating your uniqueness and following your own journey, even if it diverges from the norm. Surround yourself with people who inspire you to embrace your true self and chase your goals, regardless of societal expectations.

2. Cultural Norms: The Unseen Influence of Tradition

Cultural norms refer to the collective beliefs and practices that establish what is deemed acceptable or appropriate within a specific society or group. These norms are often deeply rooted and can be challenging to confront, as they are upheld by tradition, socialization, and peer influence.

Cultural norms can foster a sense of identity and belonging; however, they may also impose limitations. In certain cultures, there can be significant expectations regarding gender roles, career paths, or family structures that may limit personal freedom and self-expression.

To address the constraints set by cultural norms, it is essential to first recognize the norms that influence your behavior. Consider how these norms have shaped your beliefs and actions, and evaluate whether they resonate with your authentic self. Examine these norms by assessing their validity and considering different viewpoints. Explore a variety of experiences and perspectives that expand your understanding of possibilities. In doing so, you can cultivate a life that is more genuine and satisfying, aligning with your values and aspirations.

3. Economic Constraints: Understanding Financial Limitations

Economic constraints are external factors that can greatly influence your capacity to reach your objectives. These constraints encompass factors like income level, access to education, employment opportunities, and financial stability. Financial constraints can lead to considerable stress and uncertainty, hindering your ability to chase your goals or embrace new opportunities.

Although economic constraints are significant and can present challenges, they are not impossible to overcome. To overcome these limitations, it is essential to embrace a mindset of resourcefulness and resilience. Concentrate on the aspects you can influence and explore innovative methods to operate within your limitations. Look for opportunities to pursue education and develop skills that can improve your earning potential. Establish a robust support network comprising mentors, colleagues, and friends who can offer valuable guidance and encouragement.

Furthermore, fostering a positive relationship with money is essential. Understand that financial success is just one aspect of achievement and that wealth can manifest in various ways, such as personal fulfillment, relationships, and overall well-being. Redefining your concept of success allows you to discover pathways to achieve your goals, even amidst economic challenges.

4. Systemic Inequalities: Addressing the Challenge of Injustice

Systemic inequalities are structural barriers in society that can restrict opportunities for specific groups of individuals. Inequalities can arise from various factors, including race, gender, socioeconomic status, or disability, which can all contribute to inequalities. Systemic barriers can lead to considerable disadvantages, hindering individuals' access to education, employment, healthcare, and other vital resources.

Addressing systemic inequalities necessitates both personal and group efforts. At a personal level, you can support yourself and others by pursuing opportunities for education, skill enhancement, and career growth. Participate in activism and advocacy initiatives aimed at breaking down systemic barriers and fostering equality.

At a collective level, it is essential to advocate for policies and initiatives that foster social justice and equity. This could involve promoting changes in legislation and regulations, backing organizations that tackle systemic inequalities, and increasing awareness of these issues in your community.

Although systemic inequalities are deeply rooted and challenging to address, progress can be achieved when individuals and communities collaborate to foster change. Taking action can contribute to the creation of a more just and equitable society, ensuring that everyone has the opportunity to realize their full potential.

Strategies for Liberation: Empowering Yourself to Overcome

Overcoming limitations involves a blend of self-awareness, resilience, and proactive approaches. The strategies outlined below aim to assist you in overcoming personal and external barriers, enabling you to navigate challenges and reach your goals effectively.

1. Developing Self-Awareness: Recognizing Your Strengths and Weaknesses

Self-awareness serves as the cornerstone for personal development and empowerment. Understanding your strengths and weaknesses allows you to make informed decisions on how to address your limitations and reach your goals.

Begin with a comprehensive self-evaluation. Consider your previous experiences, accomplishments, and obstacles. Recognize the skills and qualities that have played a role in your success, along with the areas that require enhancement. It may be beneficial to seek feedback from trusted colleagues, mentors, or friends who can offer an objective view of your strengths and weaknesses.

After gaining a clear understanding of yourself, leverage this insight to establish realistic goals and create a plan for accomplishing them. Concentrate on utilizing your strengths while also making efforts to improve your weaknesses. Self-awareness is a continuous journey, and it is essential to regularly evaluate and refine your goals as you evolve and progress.

2. Developing Resilience: Enhancing Your Capacity to Recover

Resilience refers to the capacity to recover from difficulties and persist in progress, despite encountering obstacles. Developing resilience is crucial for surpassing obstacles and reaching your objectives.

Building resilience can be achieved by cultivating a growth mindset, which is the belief that your abilities and intelligence can improve through effort and learning. Welcome challenges as opportunities for development, and view setbacks as valuable lessons. Embrace self-compassion and acknowledge that failure is an inherent aspect of the learning journey.

A crucial element of resilience is the ability to maintain a robust support network. Engage with individuals who uplift and support you, fostering your development and helping you overcome obstacles. Participate in activities that enhance both physical and mental health, including consistent exercise, mindfulness techniques, and enjoyable hobbies.

Lastly, develop a sense of purpose that informs your actions and choices. A clear sense of purpose enhances your motivation and resilience when facing challenges. Check your values and goals to make sure your actions match them.

3. Taking Action: Conquering Inertia and Progressing

Taking action is essential for overcoming limitations and reaching your goals. Fear or uncertainty often leads to inaction, which stands as one of the greatest barriers to personal growth.

Begin by establishing small, attainable goals that can help you gain momentum and overcome inertia. Divide larger tasks into smaller, manageable steps and concentrate on achieving steady progress, even if it occurs gradually. Celebrate your achievements with positive reinforcement to motivate yourself to continue moving forward.

Establishing a routine that aligns with your goals is another crucial strategy. Develop daily or weekly routines that bring you nearer to your goals. Maintaining consistency is essential for generating momentum and breaking through inertia.

Ultimately, embrace the opportunity to take risks. Venturing beyond your comfort zone is crucial for personal development, even if it involves the risk of failure. Keep in mind that the most significant rewards frequently arise from making courageous decisions and welcoming the unknown.

4. Seeking Support: Cultivating a Network of Allies

Success is not achieved in isolation. Establishing a robust support network is crucial for overcoming challenges and reaching your objectives. A strong support network should consist of mentors, colleagues, friends, and family members who have faith in you and offer guidance, encouragement, and constructive feedback.

Begin by identifying individuals who align with your values and objectives to establish a support network. Look for mentors with experience and expertise in your field, as they can offer valuable advice and insights.

Engage with professional organizations, networking groups, or online communities to connect with individuals who share similar interests.

Feel free to seek assistance whenever necessary. Contact your support network for guidance, input, or help with particular challenges. Keep in mind that support goes both ways, and be open to providing assistance and encouragement to others.

5. Embracing Change: Adjusting to New Realities

Change is a constant factor, and the capacity to adjust to new circumstances is crucial for transcending limitations and reaching your objectives. Embracing change necessitates adaptability, receptiveness to fresh concepts, and a readiness to venture beyond your comfort zone.

To embrace change, begin by cultivating a mindset focused on continuous learning. Maintain a sense of curiosity and openness to new experiences, and be prepared to consider various perspectives. Look for opportunities to grow and develop, whether through formal education, on-the-job training, or personal exploration.

Embracing change also involves taking a proactive approach to managing your career and personal development. Keep yourself updated on the trends and developments within your industry, and be ready to adjust your skills and strategies accordingly. Stay receptive to new opportunities, even if they lead you down an unforeseen path.

Finally, engage in mindfulness and remain focused on the present moment. Change can feel daunting, yet by maintaining a focus on the present, you can approach challenges with enhanced clarity and resilience.

Conclusion: Discovering Your Inner Hero

Breaking free from limitations is an ongoing journey of self-discovery, growth, and empowerment that lasts a lifetime. By recognizing and addressing both personal and external obstacles, you can unlock your inner hero and reach your full potential.

The challenges you encounter are not impossible to overcome. By cultivating self-awareness, resilience, and a proactive mindset, you can overcome the challenges that arise in your path. Embrace the journey with confidence and resolve, and have faith in your capacity to shape the life you want.

As you progress, keep reflecting on the insights and strategies you have acquired from this chapter. Incorporate them into your daily routine, allowing them to guide you as you work towards your goals and aspirations. By overcoming limitations, you empower yourself and inspire others to follow suit. By working together, we can build a world where everyone has the chance to reach their full potential and become the hero of their own narrative.

Actionable Steps: Moving Forward

1. Recognize Your Personal Barriers: Spend some time considering the personal obstacles that may be hindering your progress, including self-doubt, fear of failure, or limiting beliefs. Document them, critically assess their validity, and consider alternative viewpoints.

2. Set Realistic Goals: Define specific, attainable objectives that resonate with your values and ambitions. Divide larger objectives into smaller, achievable tasks, and concentrate on maintaining steady progress.

3. Establish Your Support Network: Recognize individuals who can offer guidance, encouragement, and constructive feedback. Connect with potential mentors, participate in networking groups, and interact with individuals who share your aspirations.

4. Embrace Change: Remain receptive to new experiences and be prepared to adjust to evolving circumstances. Consistently look for opportunities to enhance your growth and development, and take initiative in overseeing your career and personal advancement.

5. Take Action: Break free from inertia by consistently and proactively moving toward your goals. Embrace the opportunity to take risks and venture beyond your comfort zone. Keep in mind that any progress, regardless of its size, is still a step forward.

Worksheet: Conquering Limiting Beliefs

Please use the provided worksheet to identify and confront your limiting beliefs.

1. Identify a Limiting Belief: Take a moment to write down a belief that you believe is hindering your progress. Please provide detailed information.

2. Question the Assumption: Consider the following inquiries:

- Is this belief grounded in facts or assumptions?

- What evidence do I have to challenge this belief?

- In what ways does this belief restrict my potential?

3. Reframe the Belief: Articulate the belief in a manner that empowers you and aligns with your objectives. For instance, if you hold the belief that

"I'm not good enough to succeed," consider reframing it to *"I possess the skills and determination necessary to achieve my goals."*

4. Take Action: Determine a small step you can take to implement your new, empowering belief. Please ensure that you take this step within the next week.

Regular use of this worksheet can help you shift your mindset and overcome the limiting beliefs that are holding you back.

Summary and Recap

This chapter examines the different limitations that may prevent you from reaching your full potential, such as personal barriers, external constraints, and systemic inequalities. We talked about the significance of self-awareness, resilience, and proactive strategies in addressing these limitations, offering practical steps to assist you in overcoming challenges and achieving success. Embracing change, establishing a robust support network, and taking consistent action can help you unlock your inner hero and cultivate a life that truly reflects your potential.

As you consider the insights and strategies presented in this chapter, keep in mind that the process of overcoming limitations is continuous. Keep pushing your limits, explore new avenues for development, and have confidence in your capacity to reach your objectives. In doing so, you empower yourself while also inspiring others to follow suit.

Chapter 4

COMMUNICATION AND INFLUENCE

THE IMPACT OF YOUR WORDS

I magine a time in your life when you felt fully understood, when your thoughts expressed themselves seamlessly, and when the person you were speaking with genuinely comprehended your message. That moment, whether brief or enduring, was not merely about conversation; it was about establishing a connection. Effective communication goes beyond just exchanging words; it involves connecting with others, shaping viewpoints, and fostering relationships that motivate action. In leadership, the stakes are significantly elevated. Effective communication serves as a crucial instrument for leaders to articulate visions, unite teams, and facilitate meaningful change.

Leadership goes beyond merely occupying a position of authority; it involves the capacity to steer others toward a common objective. What's the process for achieving that? By means of communication. It goes beyond merely speaking or writing; it's about the way you express your ideas, the quality of your listening, and your ability to impact those around you. In this chapter, we will delve into the complexities of communication and influence, equipping you with the tools necessary to express your ideas clearly and enhance your influence within your networks.

We will explore how communication serves as a vital leadership tool, examine the elements of effective communication, and investigate how influence transcends mere words. This chapter focuses on enhancing your communication skills while also guiding you to become a leader that others aspire to follow. Let us commence.

The Anatomy of Effective Communication

Clear communication is fundamental to effective leadership. Having a vision is just the beginning; it is essential to communicate that vision effectively so that it connects with others. What does effective communication entail?

Clarity: The Primary Foundation

Effective communication fundamentally begins with clarity. Consider the challenge of putting together a piece of furniture when the instructions are not clear—it's certainly a source of frustration. The same concept holds true for leadership. If your message is unclear, your team will lack guidance on the path forward. Clarity means breaking down intricate ideas into easily comprehensible concepts. Avoiding jargon unless absolutely necessary and selecting words that accurately convey your message is essential.

To achieve clarity:

- **Understand Your Message:** Prior to speaking or writing, ensure you are clear about what you wish to communicate. What is the main message? What are the main points you want your audience to remember?

- **Streamline Your Communication:** Complexity is not synonymous with intelligence. Clear and straightforward language frequently yields the greatest effect. Steer clear of

buzzwords or industry jargon that may disconnect segments of
your audience.

- **Organize Your Communication:** A clearly organized message
  is simpler to understand. Begin with your primary argument,
  followed by supporting evidence or examples, and finish with a
  compelling summary.

Empathy: The Connection Between People

Effective communication requires mutual engagement, and empathy
serves as the foundation for fostering understanding. Leaders who
communicate with empathy engage in dialogue not only by speaking
but also by actively listening. They take into account the emotions and
viewpoints of their audience, enhancing the effectiveness and relatability
of their communication.

Effective communication requires empathy, which includes:

- **Active Listening:** Focus on the emotions conveyed, not just
  the words themselves. When you listen, engage fully rather than
  merely anticipating your opportunity to respond. Participate
  in the conversation by listening actively, posing questions, and
  considering the answers provided.

- **Comprehending Your Audience:** Understand your audience.
  What are their concerns, aspirations, and obstacles? Customize
  your communication to align with their experiences.

- **Authenticity:** Individuals can recognize when you are not being
  sincere. Express yourself sincerely and allow your enthusiasm to
  shine through. Being genuine fosters trust, an essential element

for successful communication.

Conciseness: Less is More

In today's fast-paced environment, the importance of brevity cannot be overstated. Effective communication is a vital skill that distinguishes you as a leader. Being concise does not imply omitting essential information; rather, it involves conveying your message in the most effective manner possible.

To communicate concisely:

- **Revise Thoroughly:** Prior to conveying your message, examine it carefully and eliminate any superfluous words or phrases. Each word must have a specific purpose.

- **Stay focused:** Refrain from going off-topic or providing excessive details. Concentrate on the main message you wish to communicate and back it up with sufficient detail to make it engaging.

- **Utilize Visual Aids:** At times, an image can convey a multitude of meanings and emotions. Utilize charts, diagrams, or images when suitable to effectively and efficiently communicate complex concepts.

Confidence: The Foundation of Influence

Confidence in communication is not about being the loudest person in the room; it is about delivering your message with conviction. Confidence arises from a deep understanding of your subject, a strong belief in your message, and a willingness to embrace differing opinions.

To convey assurance:

- **Understand Your Material:** Ensure you are well-prepared and informed about the topic at hand. As your knowledge increases, so too will your confidence.

- **Maintain Eye Contact:** Maintain eye contact during face-to-face communication, as it can express confidence and sincerity. Your engagement and presence in the conversation are evident.

- **Speak Clearly and Slowly:** Articulate your words with clarity and take your time. Speaking too quickly may convey feelings of nervousness or a lack of confidence. Take your time to express your thoughts clearly.

Establishing Influence via Effective Communication

Communication serves as the essential tool for establishing influence; however, influence encompasses more than mere persuasion. It involves establishing credibility, earning trust, and possessing the capacity to motivate others to pursue your vision. Influence is not rooted in manipulation; rather, it stems from genuine connection.

Credibility: The Cornerstone of Influence

Establishing credibility is essential for influencing others. Credibility is built on a foundation of knowledge, experience, and integrity. It entails establishing yourself as a dependable, trustworthy, and competent individual.

Building credibility involves:

- **Being Consistent:** maintaining consistency in your actions and words, which fosters trust. Individuals are more inclined to follow a leader who they trust to fulfill their commitments.

- **Showcasing Proficiency:** Convey your insights and expertise to others. The more you know, the more others will seek your advice.

- **Recognizing When You Lack Knowledge:** It is important to acknowledge that no one possesses all the answers, and feigning knowledge can undermine your credibility. If you are unsure about an answer, it's important to be truthful and demonstrate a desire to learn.

Emotional Intelligence: A Crucial Element for Influence

Emotional intelligence (EI) refers to the capacity to identify, comprehend, and regulate your own emotions, along with the emotions of those around you. Leaders who possess strong emotional intelligence are adept at navigating social complexities, setting positive examples, and effectively managing conflicts.

To improve your emotional intelligence:

- **Enhance Self-Awareness:** Recognise your emotions and their influence on your actions. Consider your strengths and weaknesses, as well as how they influence your leadership style.

- **Develop Self-Regulation:** Cultivate the ability to manage your impulses and consider your actions carefully before proceeding. This aids in preserving calmness, particularly during challenging circumstances.

- **Foster Empathy:** Empathy serves as a fundamental element of emotional intelligence. Make an effort to understand others' viewpoints and experiences before arriving at decisions.

Persuasion: The Art of Gentle Influence

Persuasion involves leading others to understand your viewpoint while maintaining respect and integrity throughout the process. Persuasive communication involves sharing your ideas in a way that engages and resonates with others, rather than imposing your views on them.

In order to effectively persuade others:

- **Use Logic and Emotion:** Effective persuasion requires a harmonious blend of logic and emotion. Provide data and evidence to back your arguments while also establishing an emotional connection with your audience.

- **Share narratives:** People have an innate tendency to connect with stories. Incorporate stories and personal experiences to demonstrate your points and improve your message's relatability.

- **Identify common interests:** Recognize common ground prior to presenting your argument. Establishing trust lays the groundwork for your audience to be more receptive to your ideas.

The Role of Nonverbal Communication

Words represent just one aspect of the communication process. Nonverbal cues, including body language, facial expressions, and tone of voice, are essential in shaping the reception of your message. Nonverbal signals influence up to 93% of the effectiveness of communication, according to research. Consequently, it is crucial for any leader to master nonverbal communication.

Body Language: The Unspoken Language

Your body language can support or undermine your verbal communication. A slouched posture may suggest disinterest or a lack of confidence, whereas an open stance can convey engagement and approachability.

Key aspects of effective body language include:

- Maintain an upright posture, whether standing or sitting, to express confidence and attentiveness.

- Avoid crossing your arms to avoid appearing defensive.

- Utilize hand gestures to highlight key points while ensuring not to overuse them.

- Deliberate and measured gestures are more impactful than hasty ones.

- Facial Expressions: Make sure your facial expressions are in harmony with your message. A sincere smile can create a sense of comfort for others, whereas a frown may express dissatisfaction or disapproval.

The Tone of Voice: The Music of Speech

The tone of voice you use can significantly alter the interpretation of your words. The interpretation of the same sentence can vary significantly based on the tone in which it is expressed, whether that be with enthusiasm, sarcasm, or indifference.

To refine your tone of voice:

- **Vary your pitch:** A monotone voice can disengage listeners. Utilize inflection to highlight important points and keep the audience engaged.

- **Manage Your Volume:** Speaking too loudly may be perceived as aggressive, whereas speaking too softly can convey uncertainty. Identify a volume that conveys confidence while remaining friendly.

- **Moderate Your Speed:** Speaking too quickly may overwhelm your audience, whereas speaking too slowly can lead to disinterest. Strive for a rhythm that is straightforward yet engaging.

The Impact of Online Communication

In the current digital era, a significant portion of our communication occurs online, whether via emails, social media, or virtual meetings. Digital communication offers distinct challenges and opportunities for leaders aiming to influence others.

Email Communication Mastery

Emails serve as a fundamental means of communication in the professional realm; however, they are prone to misinterpretation because of the absence of nonverbal cues. Creating effective emails involves achieving a balance between clarity, conciseness, and the appropriate tone.

To compose effective emails:

- **Begin with a Clear Subject Line:** A thoughtfully composed subject line establishes the tone of your message and assists the recipient in prioritizing your email.

- **Be clear yet comprehensive.** Be concise and direct while including all essential details. Organize your content using bullet points or numbered lists.

- **Be mindful of your tone. In** the absence of vocal inflections or facial cues, your words may be easily misunderstood. Avoid using sarcasm, and make sure your intentions are clear.

Utilizing Social Media for Impact

Social media platforms provide leaders with a distinctive chance to reach and impact a wider audience. Nonetheless, the casual nature of these platforms necessitates an alternative approach to communication.

Effective social media communication involves:

- **Authenticity:** Be sincere in your interactions. Express your thoughts, experiences, and insights authentically.

- **Engagement:** Rather than simply broadcasting messages, focus on interacting with your audience. Engage with comments, participate in discussions, and express gratitude towards your followers.

- **Consistency:** Maintain a regular schedule of sharing content that reflects your values and expertise. Maintaining consistency strengthens your brand and enhances your credibility.

Managing Virtual Meetings

Virtual meetings have become an essential part of the modern work environment. Nonetheless, the absence of physical presence can pose challenges in forming connections and sustaining engagement.

To lead effective virtual meetings:

- **Plan Ahead:** Create a detailed agenda and distribute it to participants in advance. This allows everyone to understand what to anticipate and prepare appropriately.

- **Encourage Engagement:** In virtual environments, it's common for participants to take a passive role. Encourage everyone to participate by asking questions and accepting their feedback.

- **Be aware of time zones:** If your team is located in various time zones, please take the timing of your meetings into account. Arrange the meetings at a time that is convenient for all participants, or alternate meeting times to suit various regions.

Case Studies and Practical Examples

To enhance our understanding of communication and influence, let's examine real-life examples and case studies of leaders who have excelled in these areas.

Steve Jobs: The Strength of Simplicity

Steve Jobs was recognized for his talent in conveying intricate concepts in straightforward, relatable language. The product launches he conducted were remarkable, not only for the innovative features they highlighted but also for the manner in which Jobs delivered them. He employed clear and concise language, impactful visuals, and storytelling to ensure his message connected with his audience.

Jobs' approach to communication demonstrates the strength of simplicity. Eliminating superfluous details and concentrating on the essential message allows for a significant impact.

Oprah Winfrey: Guiding with Compassion

Oprah Winfrey's success as a media mogul and philanthropist can be attributed in part to her outstanding communication skills, especially her talent for forming emotional connections with others. Oprah engages in active listening, communicates with warmth and sincerity, and demonstrates true empathy for others.

Her approach highlights the significance of empathy in communication. When individuals feel acknowledged and comprehended, they are more inclined to be swayed and motivated by your message.

Nelson Mandela: The Impact of Integrity

Nelson Mandela's leadership was grounded in integrity and a profound commitment to justice. His capacity to articulate his vision for a free and equal South Africa, even while incarcerated, motivated millions. Mandela's speeches exemplified moral clarity and a steadfast dedication to his principles.

Mandela's life and leadership exemplify the importance of integrity in establishing influence. When your words are supported by solid values and consistent actions, individuals are more inclined to trust and follow you.

Worksheet: Developing Your Leadership Message

We have developed an activity to assist you in applying the concepts covered in this chapter, aimed at enhancing your communication and influence skills.

1. Identify Your Core Message: What is the key message you wish to communicate as a leader? Summarize it in a single sentence.

2. Clarify Your Message: Evaluate your main point. Can you simplify any complex words or phrases? Please rephrase your message using straightforward and easy-to-understand language.

3. Take Your Audience into Account: Whom are you in communication with? What are their concerns and motivations? Customize your communication to focus on these points.

4. Practice Empathy: Reflect on a recent conversation in which you felt that your perspective was not fully grasped. In what ways could you have expressed greater empathy in your communication? Please provide a revised version of that conversation.

5. Enhance Your Nonverbal Communication: Capture a recording of yourself presenting your main message. Be mindful of your body language, facial expressions, and tone of voice. What nonverbal signals are you conveying? What steps can be taken to enhance them?

6. Organize a Virtual Meeting: If you are in charge of leading virtual meetings, use this checklist to ensure thorough preparation.

- Establish a well-defined agenda.

- Make sure you have the required technology in place.

- Develop a strategy to involve participants and foster interaction.

- Please provide the meeting notes and action items for follow-up.

Completing this worksheet will help you create a more impactful leadership message that connects with your audience and improves your capacity to influence others.

Action Points: Applying What You've Learned

As you progress, keep in mind the following action points to assist you in implementing the lessons from this chapter:

1. Engage in Active Listening: During your next conversation, prioritize listening over speaking. Take a moment to consider what you've heard before providing your response.

2. Streamline Your Communication: Take a moment to assess your recent communications—be it emails, presentations, or discussions. In what areas can you streamline your language or structure to enhance clarity?

3. Improve Your Nonverbal Communication: Pay closer attention to your body language and tone during your interactions. Implement minor changes and note the effects they have on your communication.

4. Utilize Stories for Persuasion: The next time you aim to persuade someone, consider using a story to effectively illustrate your point. Observe how it alters the dynamics of the conversation.

5. Connect with Your Digital Audience: Whether via social media or email, strive to interact with your audience in a genuine manner. Engage with comments, pose questions, and express gratitude for their participation.

Conclusion: The Legacy of Your Words

As we wrap up this chapter, it is important to consider the significant influence that communication exerts on leadership. Your words can inspire, challenge, comfort, and guide others. Ultimately, it's not just about the words you choose; it's about how you engage with others, express your vision, and impact those in your sphere that shapes your legacy as a leader.

Leadership is a collaborative endeavor. The relationships you cultivate and the influence you exert collectively shape the experience. Mastering the art of communication allows you to lead while empowering others to grow alongside you.

As you progress, carry with you the insights of clarity, empathy, conciseness, and confidence. Utilize them to shape your message, enhance your influence, and guide with intention. The path to becoming a leader that others aspire to follow starts with the language you use and the relationships you cultivate.

Allow your communication to serve as a bridge that connects, a guiding light, and a spark that inspires the potential in others. By taking this approach, you will genuinely step into a leadership role.

Chapter 5

DECISION-MAKING AND RESPONSIBILITY

THE INFLUENCE OF DECISIONS

P icture yourself at a crossroads, where each path diverges towards a unique destination, and every choice shapes the course of your life. This moment, both simple and profound, captures the essence of decision-making. The decisions we make, whether significant or minor, influence our lives and establish our identities as leaders. It's not solely about making choices; it's about selecting the right ones and taking responsibility for the outcomes, whether they are positive or negative.

Leadership involves decision-making that encompasses both artistic and scientific elements. It necessitates a careful equilibrium between instinct and evaluation, between embracing risks and practicing prudence. It requires a comprehension of the significant responsibility that accompanies every decision. Effectively navigating these complexities sets outstanding leaders apart from others. This chapter thoroughly examines the decision-making process, highlighting the significance of making informed choices and the necessity of taking responsibility for those decisions. By examining real-life examples, historical insights, and practical advice, we will explore what it means to be a leader who not only makes decisions but also stands by them, embodying the integrity and accountability that motivate others to follow.

The Structure of Decision-Making

Comprehending the Decision-Making Process

Decision-making is frequently perceived as a distinct action—a specific moment when a choice is made. Nonetheless, it encompasses much more than that. The process consists of several steps, including collecting information, evaluating options, anticipating outcomes, and ultimately making a decision. Grasping this process is essential for any leader aiming to make informed decisions.

1. Identifying the Problem: The initial step in the decision-making process is acknowledging that a decision must be made. It may appear straightforward, yet in the dynamic realm of leadership, it is common to miss issues or postpone addressing them until they become more significant. Effective leaders proactively identify issues before they escalate into crises.

2. Gathering Information: After identifying a problem, the subsequent step involves collecting pertinent information. This includes gathering data, seeking advice from experts, and comprehending the context of the situation. Information overload can present challenges, making it crucial to recognize when you have sufficient data to make an informed decision.

3. Considering Alternatives: With the available information, the next step involves generating and assessing potential solutions. This demands innovative thinking and an openness to explore all options, including those that may initially appear unconventional or risky.

4. Evaluating the Consequences: Every possible solution will yield consequences—some beneficial, others detrimental. A strong leader should foresee these results and consider them thoughtfully. This step typically requires both logical analysis and intuitive judgment.

5. Making the Decision: After evaluating the options and their possible outcomes, it is now time to reach a decision. The leader's courage and confidence are crucial in this situation. Indecision can be more harmful than making an incorrect choice, as it fosters uncertainty and undermines trust.

6. Taking Action: The effectiveness of a decision is determined by how well it is executed. Effective leaders carry out their decisions, ensuring that they implement actions to achieve the chosen solution.

7. Reviewing the Decision: After executing the decision, it's crucial to evaluate its results. Was the issue resolved? Were there any unforeseen outcomes? This step offers important insights that can guide future decisions.

The Importance of Intuition in decision-making

Intuition is frequently criticized in decision-making discussions, regarded as unscientific or unreliable. Intuition, commonly known as *"gut feeling,"* plays a crucial role in decision-making, particularly in leadership. Intuition arises from years of experience and the subconscious recognition of patterns. Although data and analysis hold significant value, intuition enables leaders to make swift decisions in circumstances where information may be lacking or time is critical.

Reflect on the account of Captain Chesley *"Sully"* Sullenberger, the pilot who adeptly landed a disabled aircraft on the Hudson River in 2009. After both engines failed shortly after takeoff, Sully had only seconds to determine whether to try returning to the airport or to land in the river. His decision, which preserved the lives of all 155 individuals on board, was influenced not only by technical expertise but also by intuition developed over decades of flying experience. Sully later recounted how, in that moment, he experienced a deep sense of calm and clarity, as if his entire career had led him to that singular decision.

Intuition should not be seen as a replacement for analysis; instead, it should serve to enhance it. Leaders should trust their instincts, especially when their experience and expertise back them up. It is essential to recognize the potential biases that may affect intuition, including overconfidence and the inclination to prefer familiar choices.

Balancing Logic and Emotion

Leaders frequently encounter the challenge of finding a balance between logic and emotion when making decisions. Logic offers a clear and rational way forward, whereas emotions provide valuable insight into the human consequences of a decision. Both aspects hold significance, but it is essential to maintain a balance to prevent decisions that lean towards being overly analytical or excessively emotional.

Imagine a company that faces financial challenges and must decide whether to downsize. A strictly logical approach could suggest reducing a substantial part of the workforce to achieve cost savings. Nonetheless, a leader who accounts for the emotional and social effects of such a decision may look into alternative solutions, like temporary pay reductions or voluntary retirement packages, to lessen the adverse effects on employees.

Finding the right balance between logic and emotion can be challenging, yet it is crucial for making decisions that are both effective and compassionate. Leaders need to understand the perspectives of those impacted by their decisions while also keeping a sharp focus on the organization's long-term objectives.

Embracing Accountability: A Key Trait of Leadership

Taking Charge of Your Choices

Making decisions is just one part of the process; the other part involves taking responsibility for those choices. This involves taking responsibility for both the achievements and the setbacks that arise from your decisions. Leaders who embrace responsibility gain the trust and respect of their teams by showcasing integrity and accountability.

One notable example of a leader assuming responsibility is President Harry S. Truman, who famously displayed a sign on his desk that stated, *"The buck stops here."* This statement reflects Truman's conviction that, as President, he bore ultimate responsibility for the decisions made by his administration, regardless of their outcomes. In a leadership context, this means taking responsibility for your decisions and their consequences rather than shifting the blame onto others when problems arise.

Being accountable also means being open about how you make decisions. When a leader articulates the rationale behind their decisions, it not only aids others in comprehending and endorsing those choices but also cultivates an environment of transparency and trust. When New Zealand Prime Minister Jacinda Ardern implemented strict lockdown measures in response to the COVID-19 pandemic, she clearly articulated the rationale behind these decisions, consistently communicating with the public to explain the data and reasoning that informed her actions. The transparency fostered public trust and compliance, playing a significant role in New Zealand's effective management of the crisis.

Gaining Insights from Errors

Every leader has imperfections, and it is inevitable that they will encounter mistakes at various times. Great leaders are distinguished by their capacity to learn from mistakes and transform them into opportunities for growth. This necessitates humility, self-awareness, and a dedication to ongoing development.

The introduction of *"New Coke"* by Coca-Cola in 1985 serves as a well-known example of learning from mistakes. In an effort to compete with Pepsi, the company altered its classic formula, resulting in significant backlash from consumers. Coca-Cola executives chose to listen to their customers instead of rigidly adhering to their decision. They acknowledged their mistake and brought back the original formula, branding it as *"Coca-Cola Classic."* This action not only revitalized the company's market standing but also strengthened the brand's dedication to its customers.

Fostering an environment where team members can openly acknowledge their mistakes without the fear of repercussions is essential for learning and growth. When leaders exemplify this behavior, it inspires others to take responsibility for their actions and cultivates an atmosphere of ongoing learning and enhancement.

The Ethical Aspects of Responsibility

Leadership responsibility encompasses not only taking ownership of decisions but also ensuring that those decisions are ethically sound. Leaders should take into account the wider implications of their decisions on stakeholders, the community, and society as a whole. This necessitates a dedication to ethical principles, including fairness, honesty, and respect for others.

One of the most challenging ethical dilemmas in leadership is the tension between profit and ethics. A company may encounter the dilemma of deciding whether to compromise on product safety in order to reduce expenses. Although this may enhance short-term profits, it could lead to severe long-term repercussions regarding consumer trust and legal liability. Leaders who emphasize ethical considerations rather than immediate profits are more inclined to create sustainable and successful organizations.

The narrative surrounding Johnson & Johnson's response to the Tylenol crisis in 1982 serves as a notable illustration of ethical leadership and accountability. When multiple individuals lost their lives after consuming Tylenol capsules contaminated with cyanide, the company had the opportunity to distance itself from the crisis, given that the tampering took place after the product had left their control. Johnson & Johnson responded promptly and effectively by recalling all Tylenol products, collaborating with authorities, and creating tamper-proof packaging. This response, driven by a dedication to consumer safety, successfully rebuilt public trust and established a new benchmark for corporate responsibility.

The Ripple Effect of Responsibility

Leadership's responsibility creates a ripple effect that extends far beyond the individual leader. When leaders assume responsibility for their decisions, they establish a standard for others to emulate. This fosters a culture of accountability across the organization, ensuring that everyone recognizes their responsibility for their actions and their effects on the team and the wider community.

In organizations where leaders consistently show accountability, employees are more inclined to take ownership of their work, resulting in increased engagement, productivity, and innovation. Conversely, when leaders avoid accountability or attribute failures to others, it fosters an environment of fear and distrust, leading employees to be less inclined to take risks or put in additional effort.

The impact of responsibility also reaches the leader's influence beyond the organization. Leaders recognized for their integrity and accountability frequently act as role models within their communities, motivating others to embrace comparable values in both their personal and professional endeavors. Responsibility is not merely a personal attribute; it serves as a fundamental element of effective leadership, capable of fostering positive change that extends well beyond the leader's direct influence.

Effective Decision-Making Tools for Leaders

The Decision Matrix

The decision matrix is one of the most effective tools for making informed decisions. This tool enables leaders to methodically assess and contrast various options according to established criteria. The decision matrix helps remove bias from the decision-making process and ensures the consideration of all relevant factors.

To develop a decision matrix, adhere to the following steps:

1. Identify the options: Begin by outlining all possible solutions to the issue at hand.

2. Define the criteria: Determine the essential criteria that play a crucial role in the decision-making process. Factors may encompass cost, time, impact, feasibility, and alignment with organizational values.

3. Assign weights: Allocate a weight to each criterion according to its significance. If cost is the most significant factor, assign it a higher weight than other criteria.

4. Assess the options: Review each option based on the established criteria and assign a score for each criterion. The scores ought to indicate the extent to which each option fulfills the criteria.

5. Calculate the Weighted Scores: For each criterion, multiply the score by its corresponding weight and then sum the results for each option.

6. Make the Decision: The option with the highest total score is generally the most favorable choice; however, the leader should also take into account any qualitative factors that may not be reflected in the matrix.

The SWOT Analysis

A useful tool for decision-making is the SWOT analysis, which represents ***strengths, weaknesses, opportunities, and threats.*** This tool assists leaders in evaluating the internal and external factors that may influence a decision.

To perform a SWOT analysis:

1. Strengths: Recognize the internal strengths of the organization or team that may facilitate the decision-making process. This may encompass resources, expertise, or distinctive capabilities.

2. Weaknesses: Recognize the internal weaknesses that may impede the decision-making process. These may encompass limitations in resources, gaps in skills, or challenges within the organization.

3. Opportunities: Recognize external opportunities that the decision could leverage. These may encompass market trends, technological advancements, or strategic partnerships.

4. Threats: Recognize external factors that may influence the decision-making process. These may encompass competitors, economic conditions, or regulatory challenges.

Through the analysis of these factors, leaders can develop a thorough understanding of the context surrounding their decisions. This insight enables them to select a course of action that utilizes strengths, addresses weaknesses, takes advantage of opportunities, and reduces threats.

The OODA Loop

The OODA Loop, created by military strategist John Boyd, serves as a decision-making framework that highlights the importance of speed and adaptability. The acronym represents the steps: ***observe, orient, decide, and act.*** This tool proves to be especially beneficial in dynamic settings where swift decision-making is essential.

1. Observe: Collect information regarding the situation. This requires careful observation of the environment, recognizing important elements, and tracking any changes that occur.

2. Orient: Examine the information and grasp its significance. This step requires you to process the information using your personal experiences, biases, and knowledge.

3. Make a decision: Select the most effective course of action based on the analysis. This decision needs to be made promptly to sustain the initiative.

4. Act: Execute the decision and take the necessary steps. Following the action, return to the observation phase to evaluate the outcomes and make adjustments as needed.

The OODA Loop is a dynamic process that highlights the significance of flexibility and rapid adaptation. Leaders who excel in this approach can maintain a competitive edge and adapt effectively to swiftly evolving situations.

Practical Responsibility: Strategies for Accountability

Fostering a Culture of Accountability

Establishing a culture of accountability in an organization begins with its leader. When leaders consistently show accountability, it creates a strong example for others to emulate. Here are several strategies to foster a culture of accountability:

1. Establish Clear Expectations: Make certain that all members of the organization are aware of their roles, responsibilities, and the performance expectations placed upon them. Effective communication is crucial for fostering accountability.

2. Provide the Necessary Resources: Equipping individuals with the necessary resources for their success is the only way to achieve accountability. This encompasses offering training, resources, and assistance.

3. Promote Transparent Communication: Support a culture of open and honest dialogue within the organization. Individuals ought to feel at ease when it comes to discussing challenges, seeking assistance, and offering feedback.

4. Acknowledge and Reward Accountability: Recognize and reward individuals and teams that exhibit accountability. This highlights the significance of accountability and serves as a constructive model for others.

5. Tackle Accountability Issues: When there is a deficiency in accountability, it is essential to address it swiftly and in a constructive manner. This may include offering extra support, coaching, or, at times, making difficult decisions to tackle ongoing challenges.

Personal Accountability: Setting a Standard

Leaders who demonstrate personal accountability encourage others to follow suit. This involves being open about your own errors, gaining insights from them, and actively working towards improvement. Being personally accountable means demonstrating reliability and consistency in your actions and decisions.

A leader who commits to a project or deadline should honor that commitment, even if it requires personal sacrifices. This commitment to integrity fosters trust and respect among team members, motivating others to maintain similar standards.

Personal accountability means maintaining the same standards for yourself that you expect from others. To foster punctuality, preparedness, and professionalism within your team, it is essential to exemplify these qualities in your own work. When leaders embody their principles, they foster a culture in which accountability becomes standard practice.

Worksheet: Decision-Making and Accountability in Practice

This practical worksheet is designed to assist you in applying the concepts discussed in this chapter, guiding you through a decision-making and responsibility exercise.

Step 1: Identify a Current Decision

- Consider a decision you are currently facing in your professional or personal life. Please document the decision you are currently facing, making sure to include any relevant context.

Step 2: Collect Information

- Please provide the necessary information to facilitate an informed decision. Locate sources from which you can acquire this information and proceed to collect it.

Step 3: Explore Other Options

- Consider at least three different solutions to address the issue. List the advantages and disadvantages of each option.

Step 4: Evaluate the Consequences

- Assess the possible outcomes of each option. Evaluate the immediate and future effects, along with any ethical implications.

Step 5: Reach a Conclusion

- Please select the most appropriate course of action based on your analysis. Please provide the rationale for your decision.

Step 6: Develop an Implementation Plan

- Detail the actions you will undertake to execute your decision.

- Determine the resources required and consider any potential challenges you might encounter.

Step 7: Assume Responsibility

- Consider how you will assume accountability for the decision and its consequences.

- Think about the way you will convey the decision to others and how you will address any challenges that may come up.

Conclusion: A Legacy of Leadership

Decision-making and responsibility are intrinsically linked. A leader who makes well-informed decisions and accepts responsibility for their actions creates a lasting legacy characterized by integrity, trust, and respect. This chapter has examined the complexities of the decision-making process, highlighting the significance of harmonizing logic and emotion, as well as the ethical considerations of responsibility. It has also offered practical tools and strategies for decision-making and fostering a culture of accountability.

As you progress in your leadership journey, keep in mind that each decision you make serves as a chance to showcase your dedication to your values and your accountability to those you lead. As you face intricate business challenges, make personal decisions, or guide a team through transitions, the principles outlined in this chapter will help you make choices that embody your strengths as a leader.

Action Points

- **Utilize the decision matrix:** Implement the decision matrix tool for your upcoming significant decision. Evaluate alternatives using well-defined criteria to arrive at a knowledgeable decision.

- **Carry out a SWOT analysis:** Execute a SWOT analysis for an upcoming project or challenge. Assess strengths, weaknesses, opportunities, and threats to facilitate a comprehensive decision-making process.

- **Focus on Personal Accountability:** Select a specific aspect in which you can enhance your personal accountability. Establish a clear objective and monitor your advancement.

Final Reflection

Leadership is an ongoing journey rather than a final destination. Every decision and responsibility you make affects your journey and future generations. As you contemplate this chapter, think about how you can utilize these insights to emerge as a leader who not only makes sound decisions but also embraces responsibility for them with poise and integrity. In what ways will your decisions and the responsibilities you uphold impact the world?

Chapter 6

BUILDING RESILIENCE

THE HIDDEN STRENGTH OF RESILIENCE

I magine yourself navigating through expansive, open terrain. A storm suddenly arrives. The wind howls, rain falls heavily, and lightning flashes in the vicinity. Some individuals may feel a sense of panic, feeling overwhelmed by the intensity of the storm and uncertain about the next steps to take. Some, however, continue forward with steady hands on the wheel, skillfully navigating through the storm. These individuals are not merely enduring the storm; they are adapting to it, discovering resilience in the turmoil, and ultimately emerging on the other side, stronger and more capable. Resilience is the ability to not only endure challenges but to thrive in the face of them.

Resilience involves not only recovering from setbacks but also progressing and moving ahead. It is the ability to bounce back swiftly from challenges, to adjust in the midst of hardship, and to continue advancing despite the hurdles that life presents. In the current fast-paced and constantly evolving environment, resilience has become increasingly essential. In its absence, even minor setbacks can seem daunting. With it, we not only navigate these challenges but also flourish in their aftermath.

This chapter will delve into the essence of resilience—defining what it is, discussing its importance, and outlining ways to nurture it within ourselves. We will explore the psychological foundations of resilience, identify the strategies that promote a resilient mindset, and discover how to implement these strategies in our daily lives. By the conclusion of this chapter, you will possess a set of techniques designed to cultivate and sustain your resilience, empowering you to confront life's challenges with both courage and confidence.

The Psychology of Resilience: Comprehending the Mindset

Resilience starts with our mindset. It is a skill related to mental and emotional well-being that can be cultivated by everyone through deliberate effort and consistent practice. To foster resilience, it is essential to comprehend the psychological factors involved—what distinguishes individuals who exhibit greater resilience from those who do not?

The Growth Mindset: Viewing Challenges as Opportunities

A fundamental aspect of resilience is embracing a growth mindset, a concept that was popularized by psychologist Carol Dweck. A growth mindset refers to the belief that our abilities and intelligence can be enhanced through effort, learning, and perseverance. A fixed mindset refers to the belief that our talents and intelligence are unchangeable traits.

Adopting a growth mindset allows us to see challenges as valuable opportunities for learning and personal development. Rather than feeling disheartened by failure, we view it as a valuable lesson—an integral aspect of the journey toward success. This viewpoint is central to resilience. It enables us to view setbacks not as insurmountable challenges but as opportunities for greater achievement.

Consider Thomas Edison, who famously stated, "I have not failed. I have discovered 10,000 methods that are ineffective." His unwavering commitment to innovation, even in the face of repeated setbacks, exemplifies the growth mindset in practice. Edison's resilience extended beyond mere persistence; it encompassed his capacity to view each failure as a valuable learning experience, with every setback drawing him nearer to success.

Emotional Regulation: Navigating Stress and Challenges

A key component of resilience is emotional regulation, which refers to our capacity to manage emotions effectively, particularly during stressful circumstances. Resilient individuals experience stress and negative emotions just like anyone else, but they possess the ability to handle these feelings in a constructive manner.

Resilient individuals possess an awareness of their emotions and the triggers that influence them. They engage in mindfulness practices, which assist them in remaining anchored in the present moment, thereby preventing their emotions from becoming overwhelming.

Emotional regulation encompasses several essential strategies:

1. Cognitive Reframing: This technique focuses on altering our perception of a situation. Rather than perceiving a setback as a personal failure, we can consider it a temporary challenge or a chance to acquire new knowledge. Changing one's perspective can lessen the emotional effects of challenges and facilitate coping.

2. Stress Management Techniques: Approaches like deep breathing, meditation, and physical exercise can alleviate the physiological symptoms of stress, enabling clearer thinking and more effective responses to challenges.

Consider the case of Nelson Mandela, who endured 27 years of imprisonment during the apartheid era in South Africa. Mandela's resilience was evident not only in his survival of imprisonment but also in his ability to maintain composure and emotional stability during those years. He skillfully managed his emotions, redefined his circumstances, and emerged as a leader who inspired change not through resentment but through forgiveness and hope.

The Importance of Self-Compassion

A growth mindset and emotional regulation are important, but it is equally vital to balance them with self-compassion. Resilience involves acknowledging our challenges without being overly critical of ourselves. Rather, it requires us to practice kindness towards ourselves, particularly when situations do not unfold as we had hoped.

Self-compassion involves extending the same kindness and understanding to ourselves that we would readily provide to a friend in times of difficulty. It entails acknowledging that making mistakes, experiencing pain, and facing struggles are all part of the human experience. Self-acceptance is essential for resilience, as it enables us to recognize our challenges without being overwhelmed by them.

Psychologist Kristin Neff's research indicates that self-compassion contributes to enhanced emotional resilience, alleviating anxiety and depression while promoting a healthier, more balanced outlook on life. Practicing self-compassion increases our chances of recovering from setbacks instead of remaining in a state of self-criticism.

The Power of Purpose: Finding Meaning in Adversity

Resilience is closely connected to our sense of purpose—the conviction that our lives hold meaning and that we are striving for something beyond ourselves. A clear sense of purpose can support us through difficult times, providing the motivation to persevere even when challenges arise.

Viktor Frankl, a Holocaust survivor and psychiatrist, extensively explored the significance of discovering meaning in life, even in the most horrific circumstances. In his book Man's Search for Meaning, Frankl contends that individuals who were able to discover purpose in their suffering had a greater chance of surviving the concentration camps. This sense of purpose may not stem from lofty ambitions; it can be as straightforward as the wish to reunite with a loved one or the aspiration to make a meaningful contribution to the world.

Having a purpose gives us motivation to persevere and overcome obstacles. Connecting our daily challenges to a broader purpose or value empowers us to endure, regardless of the hardships we face along the way.

Strategies for Developing Resilience

Grasping the psychological underpinnings of resilience is the initial step; the subsequent step involves creating strategies to nurture it in our everyday lives. Developing resilience resembles the process of strengthening a muscle; it demands ongoing effort, practice, and the appropriate methods. In this discussion, we will examine effective strategies for cultivating a resilient mindset.

Establishing a Support Network: The Importance of Relationships

Resilience is frequently a shared endeavor, as no one can thrive in isolation. The connections we have with others—be it family, friends, or colleagues—are essential in fostering and sustaining resilience. A robust support network offers emotional nourishment, valuable perspective, and practical help in challenging times.

1. Building social connections: Resilient individuals consistently foster their relationships. They recognize the significance of a robust and dependable support system and dedicate time to nurturing and strengthening their relationships. Engaging in regular catch-ups with friends or pursuing mentorship opportunities creates a supportive network that can be invaluable during challenging times.

2. Seeking Help When Needed: A key aspect of resilience is the ability to recognize when assistance is needed and the bravery to request it. This could involve contacting a friend for emotional support, seeking advice from a mentor, or obtaining professional assistance from a therapist. Resilient individuals view asking for help not as a weakness but as a strength.

3. Giving Back: Notably, assisting others can enhance our own resilience. Supporting others during their times of need enhances our own sense of purpose and connection, ultimately contributing to the strengthening of our resilience. This mutual exchange fosters a supportive cycle that advantages both the giver and the receiver.

Take, for instance, the example of community resilience in the face of natural disasters. Following events such as hurricanes or earthquakes, communities that unite to support each other tend to recover more swiftly and efficiently than those that remain isolated. The strength of this collective resilience highlights the importance of relationships in navigating challenges.

Developing a Resilient Routine

While routine may appear ordinary, it serves as a significant mechanism for fostering resilience. In times of chaos, establishing a routine can offer a sense of stability and control. It provides us with a sense of stability, offering something dependable to grasp when other aspects of life seem unpredictable.

1. Daily Habits: Developing daily habits that enhance physical and mental well-being is essential for building resilience. This may encompass regular physical activity, a stable sleep routine, nutritious eating habits, and mindfulness techniques. These habits enhance our overall health and enable us to manage stress more effectively.

2. Establishing small, achievable goals: Dividing larger challenges into smaller, manageable tasks can help make them feel less overwhelming. Resilient individuals establish achievable goals, concentrating on gradual progress instead of becoming overwhelmed by the larger vision. This method supports the preservation of motivation and a feeling of achievement, even in the face of considerable challenges.

3. Embracing Flexibility: Although routines are important, adaptability is equally essential. Life is full of surprises, and resilience involves the capacity to adjust when circumstances deviate from our expectations. Resilient individuals maintain a balance between routine and flexibility, adapting their plans as necessary without becoming overly rigid or stressed by changes.

An inspiring example of resilience through routine can be observed in elite athletes. Olympians follow rigorous training regimens that enhance their physical and mental stamina. They are also aware of when to modify their routines, whether it be because of injury, alterations in competition schedules, or other unexpected circumstances. The blend of discipline and flexibility serves as a fundamental aspect of their resilience.

Cultivating Optimism: The Practice of Positive Thinking

Resilient individuals often possess a strong sense of optimism. It's not about adopting an overly optimistic outlook or overlooking life's challenges; instead, it's about sustaining hope and concentrating on the opportunities that arise, even in difficult circumstances.

1. Positive Self-Talk: The manner in which we communicate with ourselves significantly influences our resilience. Resilient individuals engage in positive self-talk, emphasizing their strengths, previous successes, and capacity to navigate challenges. They address negative thoughts through affirmations, with a focus on constructive, solution-oriented thinking.

2. Gratitude Practice: Engaging in gratitude is an effective method to foster optimism. Regularly reflecting on our gratitude allows us to redirect our attention from the challenges in our lives to the positive aspects that are flourishing. This approach does not involve ignoring problems; rather, it aids in balancing our perspective, which can enhance our resilience when confronted with challenges.

3. Visualization: Techniques for visualization can enhance optimism and resilience. By visualizing successful outcomes, we equip ourselves to confront challenges with confidence and resolve. This approach is frequently adopted by top performers, including athletes and entrepreneurs, to sustain their focus and motivation.

Winston Churchill, who guided Britain during the most challenging times of World War II, embodied a spirit of resilient optimism. In the face of significant challenges, Churchill's speeches and actions radiated hope and determination. His conviction in ultimate triumph, even when defeat appeared unavoidable, inspired an entire nation to endure the challenges of the war.

Building Resilience: Implementing Strategies in Daily Life

Developing resilience involves more than just gearing up for significant life changes; it is essential to weave resilience into our everyday routines. In this section, we examine the application of the strategies discussed in real-life, everyday contexts.

1. Addressing Workplace Setbacks: In a professional environment, setbacks such as a missed promotion, an unsuccessful project, or challenging colleagues are common occurrences. Resilient individuals concentrate on the lessons they can extract from their experiences instead of fixating on the failure. They actively seek feedback, refine their strategies, and maintain persistence in achieving their goals.

2. Navigating Personal Relationships: Relationships can often be a major source of stress, particularly when conflicts emerge. Building resilience in relationships requires active listening, empathy, and effective communication. Resilient individuals strive to address conflicts in a constructive manner, uphold a balanced perspective, and safeguard their emotional health.

3. Coping with Personal Loss: Experiencing personal loss, whether due to death, illness, or the conclusion of a relationship, is among the most difficult challenges we encounter. Resilient individuals permit themselves to experience grief and emotions while also seeking support, emphasizing their strengths, and progressively reconstructing their lives with hope and purpose.

Reflect on the journey of J.K. Rowling, who encountered many rejections prior to the successful publication of the first Harry Potter book. At her lowest point, she was a single mother relying on welfare, yet she continued to persevere, driven by her conviction in her narrative and her mission as a writer. Her resilience not only resulted in her eventual success but also served as an inspiration to millions of people around the world.

Conclusion: The Lifelong Journey of Resilience

Developing resilience is an ongoing process that spans a lifetime. It is a skill that we can always enhance and improve, regardless of our current stage in life. By grasping the psychology of resilience and applying the strategies outlined in this chapter, we can prepare ourselves to confront life's unavoidable challenges with strength, adaptability, and grace.

Resilience is essential for living a life where we not only survive but also thrive—empowering ourselves and others to navigate the challenges that lifestyle presents. It involves discovering our inner strength, that aspect of ourselves that remains resilient, consistently seeks progress, and understands how to derive significance even in challenging situations.

As you progress, keep in mind that resilience resides within you. Your approach to managing stress, your resilience in the face of setbacks, and your determination to persevere despite uncertainty are all key factors. Embarking on this journey is worthwhile, not only for the challenges you encounter today but also for the individual you will evolve into tomorrow.

Practical Strategies for Developing Resilience

1. Embrace a Growth Mindset: View failures as valuable opportunities for learning and personal development. Take a moment to think about the challenges you've faced in the past and what insights you've gained from those experiences.

2. Practice Emotional Regulation: Integrate mindfulness practices into your daily routine, including deep breathing or meditation, to effectively manage stress.

3. Build a Support Network: Enhance your connections by consistently reaching out to friends and family. Feel free to reach out for assistance whenever necessary.

4. Develop a Resilient Routine: Set up a daily schedule that incorporates habits that enhance both physical and mental well-being. Maintain a routine while allowing for adaptability to changing circumstances.

5. Foster Optimism: Engage in positive self-talk and express gratitude each day. Envisioning successful outcomes can enhance confidence when confronting challenges.

Final Reflection

As you think about the ideas and approaches presented in this chapter, take a moment to consider how you can begin fostering resilience in your life starting today. What challenges are you currently encountering, and in what ways can you utilize the principles of resilience to address them? Keep in mind that resilience involves not evading challenges but rather developing the ability to flourish in spite of them. By embracing resilience, you are not merely getting ready for the next challenge; you are taking charge of your own narrative.

Chapter 7

LEADING WITH INTEGRITY

L eadership encompasses various dimensions, and although numerous qualities enhance a leader's effectiveness, integrity stands out as a fundamental and universally esteemed attribute. Integrity in leadership goes beyond merely speaking the truth; it involves aligning actions with fundamental values, building trust, and upholding credibility, even in challenging or inconvenient situations. It serves as a quiet influence that directs choices, molds cultures, and motivates individuals to follow—not from duty but from admiration and faith in the leader's vision.

In a landscape frequently overshadowed by scandals, corruption, and unethical conduct, the demand for leaders who embody integrity is more critical than ever. Leadership is fundamentally rooted in trust, which is cultivated through consistent and ethical actions. This chapter examines the core principles of integrity in leadership, highlighting its impact on decision-making, the establishment of credibility, and its role in shaping the success and legacy of leaders.

We will explore the fundamental principles that characterize integrity, analyze the influence of ethical leadership on both organizations and individuals, and offer practical guidance on fostering and sustaining integrity in leadership positions. Throughout this journey, we will reference historical examples, case studies, and real-life experiences to demonstrate the significant impact that integrity has on effective leadership.

The Fundamental Principles of Integrity in Leadership

Alignment Between Words and Actions

Integrity in leadership fundamentally involves a consistent alignment between a leader's words and actions. The consistency between words and actions forms the foundation of trust. When leaders consistently honor their commitments, they showcase reliability and cultivate a reputation for honesty and dependability.

Leaders who possess integrity recognize that their actions convey a stronger message than their words. They take promises seriously, and when they make one, they are committed to fulfilling it with great effort. This consistency establishes a stable environment in which followers understand what to expect, minimizing uncertainty and promoting a sense of security.

Mahatma Gandhi's leadership is frequently regarded as a prime example of integrity. Gandhi's principle of Satyagraha, or truth-force, transcended mere philosophy; it embodied a comprehensive way of life. His dedication to non-violence, even when confronted with severe opposition, was a compelling illustration of the alignment between actions and values. His leadership was credible because he embodied the principles he advocated. Gandhi not only advocated for peace; he lived it in every facet of his existence, gaining the trust and respect of millions.

Ethical Decision-Making

Leaders frequently encounter challenging decisions, particularly in circumstances where the ethical choice is not the simplest or most lucrative option. Integrity in leadership means making decisions that are not only advantageous in the short term but also ethically sound and sustainable over time. This involves taking into account the wider effects of decisions on individuals, communities, and the environment.

Making ethical decisions necessitates a profound comprehension of personal values and the bravery to uphold them, even in the face of considerable pressure to yield. Leaders who demonstrate integrity focus on long-term ethical considerations rather than immediate benefits, recognizing that unethical decisions can result in a loss of trust, legal repercussions, and harm to their reputation.

An illustrative case is that of Merck & Co., a global pharmaceutical company that decided to withdraw its arthritis drug Vioxx from the market in 2004, despite the drug being a major revenue generator. The decision followed studies that indicated Vioxx raised the risk of heart attacks and strokes. Merck's leadership decided to prioritize patient safety over profits, showcasing a commitment to ethical decision-making. While the decision posed short-term financial challenges, it ultimately safeguarded the company's integrity and credibility over time.

Clarity and Accessibility

Transparency is an essential element of integrity. Leaders who demonstrate transparency in their actions and decisions foster trust by revealing that they have nothing to conceal. This transparency promotes a culture of accountability, ensuring that everyone comprehends the rationale behind decisions and feels assured that they are made with the organization's and its stakeholders' best interests in mind.

Being transparent also means acknowledging errors. Leaders who possess integrity embrace the acknowledgment of their mistakes, viewing these instances as valuable opportunities for growth and learning. By openly discussing their shortcomings, they foster a culture that values honesty and creates a safe environment for others to recognize and learn from their own mistakes.

An illustration of transparency in leadership is evident in how New Zealand's Prime Minister Jacinda Ardern managed the COVID-19 pandemic. Ardern's government consistently offered clear and regular updates to the public, outlining the reasoning behind their decisions while being transparent about the challenges and uncertainties they faced. The transparency fostered public trust and adherence to health measures, demonstrating that openness can serve as a significant asset for leaders.

Accountability

Being accountable for one's actions is also a key aspect of integrity. Leaders who demonstrate integrity accept accountability for both their achievements and their shortcomings. They take responsibility and focus on finding solutions rather than shifting blame or making excuses when challenges arise.

Accountability is intricately linked to credibility. When leaders acknowledge their mistakes and take action to correct them, they show their dedication to doing what is right, even in challenging situations. This dedication enhances their credibility and builds trust among their teams and organizations.

An illustrative instance of accountability in leadership is President John F. Kennedy's reaction to the unsuccessful Bay of Pigs invasion in 1961. Rather than placing blame on others, Kennedy accepted full responsibility for the situation, remarking, "Victory has a hundred fathers, and defeat is an orphan." By embracing accountability, Kennedy maintained his integrity and ultimately enhanced his leadership.

Courage to Stand Up for What's Right

Integrity frequently demands bravery—the bravery to advocate for what is right, even in the face of unpopularity or risk. Leaders who possess integrity remain steadfast, unaffected by public opinion, personal interests, or external influences. They continue to uphold their values with unwavering dedication, even when confronted with challenges.

This courage is demonstrated by leaders who confront injustice, who voice their opinions when others choose silence, and who make difficult choices that reflect their ethical values. Leaders like these motivate others to uphold integrity, fostering a ripple effect that has the potential to transform both organizations and societies.

An example of this is whistleblower Edward Snowden, who disclosed extensive surveillance activities conducted by the U.S. National Security Agency (NSA). Despite the personal risks involved, Snowden decided to disclose information that he believed infringed upon the public's right to privacy. His actions ignited a worldwide discussion and highlighted the significance of upholding one's principles, even when it comes with substantial personal sacrifice.

The Influence of Ethical Leadership on Organizations and Individuals

Fostering Trust and Credibility

Trust serves as the foundation of effective leadership, while integrity enhances the worth of that trust. When leaders consistently demonstrate integrity, they foster trust among their teams, organizations, and communities. Trust is crucial not only for effective leadership but also for the success and sustainability of any organization.

Leadership founded on trust fosters a positive organizational culture, enabling individuals to feel secure, appreciated, and inspired to excel in their performance. When employees trust their leaders, they are more likely to be engaged, productive, and loyal. This trust also encompasses external stakeholders, including customers, investors, and partners, who are more inclined to support an organization perceived as ethical and reliable.

Credibility, which is closely related to trust, is an essential result of integrity in leadership. Leaders recognized for their credibility tend to have a greater impact on others, secure backing for their initiatives, and guide their organizations to success. Consistent and ethical actions build credibility, and failing to uphold integrity can rapidly diminish it.

Improving Organizational Culture

Leaders establish the atmosphere for the culture within an organization. When leaders demonstrate integrity, they foster a culture rooted in honesty, transparency, and ethical conduct. The culture shapes employee interactions, decision-making processes, and the organization's perception both within and outside its walls.

An ethical organizational culture draws in and keeps talent as employees seek workplaces where they feel respected, valued, and in harmony with the organization's values. It also decreases the chances of unethical behavior, as employees are more inclined to emulate the example established by their leaders.

Paul O'Neill, the former CEO of Alcoa, is frequently recognized as a leader who significantly transformed organizational culture by emphasizing integrity. Upon assuming leadership at Alcoa, O'Neill prioritized worker safety, a choice that faced skepticism from Wall Street. O'Neill's steadfast dedication to safety, which exemplifies his integrity, resulted in notable enhancements in Alcoa's safety record and ultimately contributed to its financial success. By placing ethics above immediate profits, O'Neill fostered a culture of trust and accountability that became fundamental to the company's success.

Encouraging Ethical Conduct in Others

Leadership carries a significant influence, and leaders who demonstrate integrity motivate others to engage in ethical behavior. When leaders demonstrate integrity, they establish a standard that others are inclined to emulate. This influence impacts not only on the leader's immediate circle but also on the wider organization and society as a whole.

Ethical leaders shape behavior by the way they act, make decisions, and communicate. They emphasize the importance of ethical behavior and foster an environment where individuals feel safe and encouraged to voice their ethical concerns. This influence aids in preventing unethical behavior, minimizing the risk of scandals and legal complications, while promoting a culture of integrity.

Anita Roddick, the founder of The Body Shop, serves as a notable example of this influence through her leadership. Roddick earned recognition for her unwavering commitment to ethical business practices, encompassing fair trade, environmental sustainability, and animal rights. Her leadership motivated a generation of entrepreneurs and consumers to emphasize ethics in business, playing a significant role in the growth of the ethical consumerism movement.

Long-Term Organizational Success

Integrity in leadership may not always yield immediate results, but it is essential for achieving long-term success. Organizations that emphasize ethical leadership tend to develop robust, sustainable businesses capable of enduring challenges over time. These organizations experience elevated levels of trust, loyalty, and support from employees, customers, and various stakeholders.

Conversely, organizations with leaders who do not demonstrate integrity frequently encounter serious difficulties, such as legal problems, harm to their reputation, and a decline in trust. Overcoming these challenges can be quite difficult and may ultimately result in the organization's decline or failure.

The downfall of Enron in 2001 highlights the serious repercussions that can arise from a deficiency of integrity in leadership. The leaders of Enron participated in unethical practices, such as accounting fraud, to artificially boost the company's profits and stock price. The exposure to these practices resulted in the company's rapid downfall, causing substantial financial losses for both employees and investors, as well as a loss of trust in corporate America. The Enron scandal underscored the critical role of integrity in leadership and the severe repercussions that can arise when it is lacking.

Cultivating and Maintaining Integrity in Leadership

Self-Reflection and Self-Awareness

Integrity starts with introspection and an understanding of oneself. Leaders should possess a profound awareness of their values, strengths, and weaknesses. This self-awareness enables individuals to recognize situations where they might be inclined to compromise their integrity and to formulate strategies for upholding their ethical standards.

Consistent self-reflection enables leaders to remain true to their values and make intentional choices that demonstrate their dedication to integrity. It also assists them in identifying when they might be deviating from their principles, enabling them to take corrective measures before their integrity is at risk.

Leaders can enhance their self-awareness by engaging in practices like journaling, meditation, or obtaining feedback from trusted colleagues or mentors. These practices assist leaders in remaining grounded and concentrated on their dedication to integrity.

Seeking Feedback and Accountability

Leaders who demonstrate integrity actively seek feedback from others and take responsibility for their actions. They recognize their own fallibility and acknowledge that feedback from others is crucial for both personal and professional development.

Gathering feedback from employees, peers, and mentors enables leaders to recognize blind spots and identify areas where their integrity might be at risk. It also shows a sense of humility and an openness to learning and growth.

Accountability is an essential component of upholding integrity. Leaders ought to implement accountability systems, including regular check-ins with a mentor or coach, to ensure they remain aligned with their values and commitments. Leaders who hold themselves accountable strengthen their dedication to integrity and foster trust with their teams.

Continuous Learning and Development

Integrity in leadership is an evolving quality that necessitates ongoing learning and growth. It is essential for leaders to remain knowledgeable about ethical considerations, best practices, and new developments within their industry. They should also be open to adjusting their approach as they gain experience and develop.

Ongoing learning enables leaders to remain true to their values and make well-informed decisions that demonstrate their dedication to integrity. It also assists them in anticipating and navigating ethical challenges that may emerge during their leadership journey.

Leaders can pursue ongoing learning by engaging in formal education, reading, attending conferences and workshops, or participating in leadership development programs. When leaders prioritize their own development, they set a strong example for others and showcase their dedication to integrity.

Establishing a Support Network

Maintaining integrity in leadership can be difficult, particularly when confronted with tough choices or outside influences. Establishing a support network of reliable colleagues, mentors, and advisors can assist leaders in remaining aligned with their values and upholding their integrity.

A support network serves as a valuable resource for navigating challenging decisions, providing guidance and perspective, while also ensuring that leaders remain accountable for their actions. It provides emotional support during difficult times, helping leaders manage the pressures and stresses of leadership.

Leaders ought to build connections with those who align with their dedication to integrity and who will encourage them to remain faithful to their principles. These relationships can play a crucial role in assisting leaders in upholding their integrity over time.

Leading by Example

Ultimately, leaders should set a positive example for others to follow. Integrity cannot be delegated or outsourced; it must be evident in a leader's actions, decisions, and communication. Leaders who exemplify integrity motivate others to engage in ethical actions and foster an environment where such behavior is standard.

Leading by example requires making ethical choices, maintaining transparency and openness, taking personal accountability, and advocating for what is right. It also entails showing respect and fairness to others, even in challenging circumstances.

When leaders consistently demonstrate integrity, they cultivate trust and credibility, promote a positive organizational culture, and inspire others to follow suit. This ultimately results in enduring success and a significant legacy.

In conclusion

Integrity serves as the foundation of effective leadership. This quality forms the foundation of trust, credibility, and ethical conduct. Leaders who demonstrate integrity motivate others to follow, not by force or power but by earning respect and fostering belief in their vision. They establish organizations that are both successful and committed to ethical practices, sustainability, and earning respect.

This chapter has examined how integrity in leadership encompasses the alignment of words and actions, ethical decision-making, transparency, accountability, and the bravery to advocate for what is right. It significantly affects both organizations and individuals, shaping the culture within organizations, influencing ethical conduct, and playing a key role in achieving long-term success.

Maintaining integrity in leadership involves self-reflection, actively seeking feedback, committing to continuous learning, establishing a support network, and exemplifying the values you wish to promote. While it may present challenges, it is crucial for leaders aiming to foster positive and enduring change.

As you contemplate the insights from this chapter, think about how you can implement these principles in your own leadership journey. What are your core values, and how do they affect behaviour? What are effective ways to establish trust and credibility with your team? How can you maintain integrity in your leadership, especially when confronted with challenges and adversity?

Action Points

1. Reflect on your values: Dedicate some time to pinpoint your fundamental values and evaluate how they correspond with your approach to leadership. Commit to upholding these values, even in challenging situations.

2. Regularly Seek Feedback: Create a consistent practice of obtaining feedback from your colleagues, team members, and mentors. Utilize this feedback to pinpoint areas that require enhancement and to ensure you remain accountable.

3. Dedicate Yourself to Ongoing Learning: Keep yourself updated on ethical considerations and best practices within your field. To improve your leadership abilities and uphold your dedication to integrity, commit to ongoing learning.

4. Establish a Support Network: Foster connections with those who are equally dedicated to upholding integrity. Leverage this support network to address challenges while remaining aligned with your values.

5. Set an example: Show integrity in your actions, decisions, and communication. Set an example and cultivate a culture that values and acknowledges ethical behavior.

Final Reflection

Leading with integrity involves more than simply doing what is right; it requires staying true to oneself and adhering to one's values. It involves building a legacy that others can respect and strive to emulate. As you progress in your leadership journey, keep in mind that integrity is not a final goal but an ongoing process of ensuring your actions reflect your values. Leading with integrity not only brings about success but also encourages others to follow suit.

Chapter 8

CREATING A VISION FOR SUCCESS

CRAFTING THE BLUEPRINT FOR YOUR FUTURE

Picture yourself on a wide, open plain as a new day begins. The horizon unfolds ahead, brimming with limitless opportunities. The decisions you make today will shape whether you stay in your current situation, feeling adrift in uncertainty, or move confidently toward a destination that aligns with your true self. Creating a vision for success is about embarking on a journey that goes beyond merely achieving a goal; it is about crafting a life that resonates with your core values and aspirations.

In the journey of leadership and personal development, possessing a clear vision is not merely a luxury; it is essential. Without a vision, we resemble ships lost at sea, exposed to the unpredictable nature of external influences. Having a vision allows us to take charge of our own destiny, steering our lives with purpose and intention. This chapter will examine the significant value of establishing a vision for success, providing you with the tools and insights necessary to define, refine, and pursue a vision that is distinctly your own.

As we explore this topic, you will discover how to align your goals with your values, crafting a roadmap for success that is both attainable and profoundly satisfying. We will examine how to establish clear, actionable goals that act as stepping stones toward your vision, as well as how to sustain the focus and resilience required to accomplish them.

Throughout this journey, we will utilize historical examples, case studies, and practical exercises to firmly ground the concepts we discuss in real-world application, avoiding a purely theoretical approach.

The Importance of Vision: Understanding Its Significance

To establish a vision for success, it is crucial to first comprehend the significance of having a vision. A vision serves as your guiding principle, directing your choices and behaviors. It offers guidance, assisting you in prioritizing what genuinely matters amid the distractions and chaos of daily life.

The Historical Significance of Vision

Throughout history, the most remarkable leaders and innovators have consistently demonstrated a clear and compelling vision. Reflect on Martin Luther King Jr., whose aspiration for a world devoid of racial injustice not only inspired a movement but also transformed the trajectory of history. His renowned "I Have a Dream" speech served not only as a call to action but also as a compelling vision of a future that countless individuals could embrace and work towards. King's vision was remarkably influential, inspiring individuals around the globe for generations beyond his era.

In a similar vein, reflect on the narrative of Steve Jobs, the co-founder of Apple Inc. Jobs envisioned a future where technology would be intuitive and accessible to all, a goal that appeared nearly unattainable at that moment. This vision influenced every decision he made, from product design to marketing strategy, ultimately resulting in the creation of some of the most iconic and user-friendly devices in history. Jobs' vision extended beyond merely selling products; it aimed to transform how individuals engage with technology and, consequently, the world around them.

These examples demonstrate the significant impact of vision. A clear vision can motivate not just yourself but also those in your vicinity, fostering collaborative efforts toward a shared objective. This serves as a powerful motivator that brings people together, offering clear direction during uncertain times.

Vision and Goals: Clarifying the Distinction

It is essential to distinguish between a vision and goals, as these concepts are frequently misunderstood. A vision represents a comprehensive view of how you envision your life or career in the future. It addresses the inquiry, "Where do I wish to go?" Goals are the specific, measurable actions you undertake to achieve your objectives. They respond to the inquiry, "How will I reach my destination?"

Consider your vision as the final destination on a map, while your goals represent the path you follow to get there. Without a clear vision, your goals may lack direction, causing you to move in circles instead of progressing forward. On the other hand, without goals, your vision stays an elusive dream, missing the concrete steps required to bring it to fruition.

The Emotional Influence of Vision

A compelling vision connects deeply on an emotional level. It's not solely about your goals, but rather the significance they hold for you. The emotional connection is essential as it offers the motivation and resilience required to navigate challenges. When your vision is in harmony with your core values and passions, it serves as a source of inner strength, guiding you through challenges and setbacks.

Take, for example, Nelson Mandela, whose aspiration for a liberated and democratic South Africa kept him resilient during 27 years of incarceration. Mandela's vision went beyond a mere political goal, deeply rooted in his principles of equality, justice, and human dignity. His deep emotional connection to his vision provided him with the strength to withstand unimaginable hardships and ultimately guide his country to freedom.

Aligning Your Vision with Your Values

For a vision of success to be genuinely impactful, it should resonate with your fundamental values. Values represent the principles and beliefs that steer your decisions and actions. Your vision is built upon their foundation.

Recognizing Your Fundamental Values

To align your vision with your values, the first step is to clearly identify what those values are. This process necessitates thorough self-reflection and transparency. Begin by considering the times in your life when you experienced the greatest sense of fulfillment and contentment. What activities were you engaged in during those times? Which values were you upholding?

If you find fulfillment in assisting others, your fundamental values may encompass compassion, service, and community. If you experienced the most joy while creating something new, your values may encompass creativity, innovation, and independence.

It is equally important to reflect on instances when you experienced dissatisfaction or a lack of fulfillment. Which values did you overlook or disregard during those periods? This can offer additional understanding of what is essential to you.

After identifying your core values, document them and place them in a visible location. Your values will act as a guiding compass, helping you to shape your vision and establish your goals.

Crafting a Vision Statement

Keeping your core values in focus, the next step is to create a vision statement—a brief expression of your aspirations for the future. This statement aims to inspire and motivate, encapsulating the core of your aspirations and the significance they hold for you.

As you develop your vision statement, reflect on these questions:

- What vision do I have for my life in the next 5, 10, or 20 years?

- What legacy do I want to leave behind?

- What influence do I aspire to have on others and the world around me?

- In what ways do my core values influence my vision for the future?

A vision statement must be clear, specific, and evoke an emotional response. It should create a clear and inspiring vision of the future you wish to achieve, one that energizes and drives you forward.

If creativity is one of your core values, your vision statement could be: "To lead a life of creative expression, inspiring others through my art and innovation, while constantly pushing the limits of what is achievable."

This statement is both aspirational and personal, embodying your distinct values and goals.

Aligning Your Vision with Your Life

After you have developed your vision statement, the subsequent step is to ensure it aligns with your present life. This entails evaluating your present circumstances and pinpointing areas where there is a gap between your vision and the actual situation.

Begin by reflecting on the following questions:

- Which elements of my life are in harmony with my vision at this moment?

- Which areas of my life are at odds with my vision?

- What adjustments should I consider to align my life with my vision?

This process may involve making challenging decisions and compromises. If your goal is to embrace a life filled with creativity and innovation, yet you find yourself in a role that limits your creative potential, it might be time to explore a career transition. If your vision includes making a positive impact on your community, but your current lifestyle limits your ability to volunteer, it may be time to reevaluate your priorities.

Keep in mind that aligning your life with your vision is not focused on achieving perfection; rather, it is about making progress. Even minor adjustments can lead to substantial effects over time, guiding you toward the life you aspire to achieve.

Setting and Achieving Goals Aligned with Your Vision

Once you have a clear vision established, the subsequent step is to define and pursue goals that will assist you in bringing that vision to fruition. This process entails deconstructing your vision into practical steps and forming a roadmap that will lead you toward success.

The SMART Framework for Setting Goals

Utilizing the SMART framework is one of the most effective methods for setting goals. SMART is an acronym that represents *specific, measurable, achievable, relevant, and time-bound*. This framework guarantees that your objectives are well-defined, achievable, and in harmony with your vision.

- **Specific:** Your goals need to be well-defined and precise, addressing the questions of what, why, and how. Instead of establishing a vague goal such as "improve my health," aim for a specific target like "exercise for 30 minutes, five times a week."

- **Measurable:** Your goals should include measurable outcomes, enabling you to monitor your progress and maintain motivation. If your goal is to write a book, you could track your progress by aiming to write 500 words each day.

- **Achievable:** Your goals should be realistic and attainable based on your current resources and limitations. Challenging yourself is essential; however, establishing overly ambitious goals may result in frustration and burnout.

- **Relevant:** Your goals must align with your vision and be consistent with your core values. If your vision is to live a life of service, then establishing a goal to volunteer 10 hours each month would be particularly pertinent.

- **Time-bound:** Your goals should include a specific deadline or timeframe, fostering a sense of urgency and aiding in maintaining your focus. For instance, rather than stating, "I'll start a new business someday," establish a clear deadline such as "launch my new business by the end of this year."

Employing the SMART framework guarantees that your goals are clearly defined, actionable, and in harmony with your overarching vision.

Breaking Down Big Goals into Manageable Steps

Ambitious goals can frequently seem daunting, particularly when they signify major transformations in your life. Breaking them down into smaller, more achievable steps can make them easier to manage.

If your objective is to launch a new business, you could consider dividing it into these steps:

- **Research and Planning:** During the initial month, focus on researching your business concept, performing market analysis, and creating a comprehensive business plan.

- **Secure Funding:** In the second month, prioritize securing funding through savings, loans, or investors.

- **Develop Your Brand:** During the third month, focus on establishing your brand by designing a logo, creating a website, and producing marketing materials.

- **Prepare for Your Business Launch:** By the fourth month, you will be equipped to launch your business, with an emphasis on marketing and acquiring customers.

Breaking down your goals into smaller steps makes them less intimidating and more achievable. Every step serves as a significant milestone on your path to realizing your vision.

Maintaining Focus and Resilience

Despite having a clear vision and well-defined goals, the path to success is seldom straightforward. Challenges and setbacks are a natural part of life, and staying focused and resilient is essential for overcoming them.

Regularly revisiting your vision and goals is an effective way to maintain focus. Reflect on the reasons for setting these goals initially, and consider how they relate to your values and vision. This can assist in rekindling your motivation and maintaining your focus.

Another important aspect of resilience is fostering a growth mindset—the belief that challenges provide opportunities for learning and personal development. Rather than perceiving setbacks as failures, consider them as opportunities for learning and growth. This perspective not only aids in recovering from challenges but also fosters ongoing growth and development.

Reflect on the journey of Thomas Edison, who encountered numerous failures before ultimately achieving success with the invention of the light bulb. When asked about his failures, Edison reportedly said, "I have not failed." I have discovered 10,000 methods that are ineffective. This unwavering determination, fueled by a distinct vision, ultimately resulted in one of the most important inventions in history.

Accountability and Support

Being accountable and having support are essential components in reaching your objectives. Sharing your goals with others increases your likelihood of staying committed and following through. Consider seeking an accountability partner, participating in a mastermind group, or sharing your progress with friends and family.

Furthermore, reaching out to mentors, coaches, or peers can offer essential guidance and support. These individuals can provide new insights, assist you in overcoming challenges, and share in your achievements throughout the journey.

Keep in mind that you are not required to pursue your vision by yourself. Being part of a supportive community can enhance your experience and improve your likelihood of achieving success.

Vision in Action: Practical Examples and Case Studies

To further demonstrate the impact of vision, let's examine some real-life examples and case studies of individuals who have effectively developed and pursued a vision for success.

Case Study: Elon Musk and His Vision for Space Exploration

Elon Musk, the founder of SpaceX, exemplifies an individual who has chased a daring and ambitious vision. Musk's vision is remarkable: to make space travel accessible to all and ultimately establish a colony on Mars.

When Musk initially shared this vision, a significant number of people expressed skepticism. For a long time, space travel was primarily the responsibility of government agencies such as NASA, making the notion of a private company taking the lead appear unlikely. Nonetheless, Musk remained resolute. He established clear objectives, including lowering the costs associated with space travel and creating reusable rockets, and systematically pursued their achievement.

SpaceX is a prominent figure in the space industry today, having achieved successful launches for numerous missions and facilitating astronaut transportation to the International Space Station. Musk's vision, once viewed as unattainable, has now become a reality, showcasing the effectiveness of a clear and compelling vision paired with unwavering determination.

Case Study: Oprah Winfrey and the Vision of Empowerment

Oprah Winfrey's journey to success exemplifies the significant influence of having a clear vision. Born into poverty and confronted with various challenges, Winfrey could have easily given in to her circumstances. She envisioned a life that went beyond her immediate surroundings—a life filled with empowerment and influence.

Winfrey's vision extended beyond personal achievement; it focused on leveraging her platform to inspire and empower others. This vision has been a guiding force in her career, spanning from her beginnings in television to her emergence as one of the most influential media moguls globally.

Through her talk show, Oprah's Book Club, and her philanthropic efforts, Winfrey has consistently leveraged her influence to uplift others, aligning her actions with her vision of empowerment. Her story exemplifies the transformative power of a vision grounded in core values and a dedication to creating a positive impact on the world.

Worksheets and Activities: Realizing Your Vision

Having delved into the concepts and examples of crafting a vision for success, it's now time to apply your knowledge in practice. The worksheets and activities provided aim to assist you in clarifying your vision, establishing aligned goals, and initiating the journey toward realizing your dreams.

Activity 1: Vision Statement Worksheet

Utilize this worksheet to develop your personal vision statement. Please respond to the following questions to help clarify your thoughts:

- What are my fundamental principles?

- What kind of influence do I aspire to have on the world?

- How do I envision my ideal life in 5, 10, or 20 years?

- In what ways do my values influence my vision for the future?

- What do I hope to be remembered for?

After addressing these questions, consolidate your answers into a clear and succinct vision statement that reflects your aspirations for the future.

Activity 2: Goal Setting Worksheet

Utilize the SMART framework to establish goals that are specific, measurable, achievable, relevant, and time-bound, ensuring they align with your vision. Begin by placing your vision statement at the top of the worksheet, and then decompose it into smaller, actionable goals.

For every objective, please provide a response to the following:

- What do I specifically aim to accomplish? What methods will I use to assess my progress?

- Is this goal realistic and achievable considering my current resources?

- How does this goal connect with my vision and values? Relevant

- What is the timeline for reaching this objective? Time-sensitive

Activity 3: Accountability and Support Plan

Develop a strategy for maintaining accountability and obtaining support throughout your journey. Please respond to the questions below:

- Whom should I share my goals with to ensure accountability?

- What type of support would be most beneficial for me (mentorship, coaching, peer group)?

- What methods can I use to monitor and acknowledge my progress?

- What challenges do I foresee, and what strategies will I employ to address them?

Conclusion: The Journey to Success

Developing a vision for success is not a singular event; it is a continuous journey of reflection, adaptation, and personal growth. Your vision will develop over time as you grow and your circumstances shift, yet its essence—your values and aspirations—will continue to serve as your guiding light.

In this chapter, we have examined the significance of having a vision, the method of aligning that vision with your values, and the steps necessary to set and accomplish goals that realize your vision. We have examined real-life examples of individuals who have effectively pursued their visions and offered practical tools and activities to assist you in doing the same.

As you progress, keep in mind that the path to success is not always straightforward. Challenges and setbacks may arise, but with a clear vision and the appropriate mindset, you can effectively navigate these obstacles and keep progressing toward the future you seek. Maintain your focus on your vision, uphold your values, and consistently work towards your goals. Your vision for success is attainable—it's your responsibility to turn it into reality.

Action Points

- **Consider Your Values:** Dedicate time to recognize your fundamental values and their impact on your future vision.

- **Develop Your Vision Statement:** Create a clear and concise vision statement that inspires and motivates you.

- **Establish SMART Goals:** Implement the SMART framework to define goals that are specific, measurable, achievable, relevant, and time-bound, ensuring they align with your vision.

- **Maintain Accountability:** Communicate your goals with a reliable friend, mentor, or peer group to ensure you remain focused.

- **Seek Support:** Surround yourself with a community that both encourages and challenges you to achieve your full potential.

Regularly assess your vision and goals, making necessary adjustments to ensure they remain in harmony with your values and aspirations.

Final Reflection

As you conclude this chapter, pause to consider the path that lies ahead. Reflect on how the vision you establish today will influence the individual you evolve into tomorrow. What actions will you implement this week, this month, and this year to progress toward your vision? In what ways will you maintain your values while working towards your objectives?

Your vision serves as a powerful guide, helping you navigate life's uncertainties and driving you toward the success you seek. Embrace it, nurture it, and allow it to guide you toward the future you have always envisioned.

Chapter 9

EMPOWERING OTHERS

In a world where leadership is frequently associated with authority and control, the idea of empowerment may appear revolutionary. True leadership is not about exercising power; it is about sharing it—empowering others to reach their fullest potential. This chapter, *"Empowering Others,"* focuses on how you, as a leader, can cultivate a culture of growth and development. By unlocking the potential of those around you, you can transform your environment into a thriving ecosystem characterized by innovation, creativity, and mutual support.

Empowerment transcends being just a buzzword; it represents a philosophy that has the potential to transform our approach to leadership, mentoring, and coaching. Embracing this mindset allows us to foster enduring change, impacting both our professional lives and our communities, as well as our personal relationships. This chapter explores the principles of empowerment, providing practical insights on effective mentoring and coaching techniques. You will learn how to nurture talent, build trust, and inspire confidence while fostering a culture where everyone feels valued and motivated to contribute.

The Influence of Empowerment: A Fresh Approach to Leadership

Empowerment in leadership involves redirecting attention from the leader to the team, transitioning from control to collaboration, and moving from command to encouragement. This method might appear unconventional, particularly in settings where established hierarchies have been prevalent for an extended period. Research and real-world examples consistently demonstrate that empowered teams exhibit greater innovation, higher engagement, and ultimately achieve greater success.

An Evolution in Leadership Models

The idea of empowerment has been around for some time. It has its origins in a variety of leadership models that have developed over the centuries. During the early 20th century, figures such as Mary Parker Follett promoted the concept of "power with" instead of "power over" individuals, marking a significant shift from the prevailing authoritarian leadership styles of that era. Follett's ideas, while pioneering, established the foundation for contemporary notions of collaborative leadership and empowerment.

With the evolution of the work environment, especially in the post-industrial era, it became increasingly clear that leadership requires a tailored approach rather than a uniform strategy. The traditional, hierarchical structures of the past have come to be viewed as barriers to innovation and creativity. A new leadership paradigm began to emerge, focusing on the significance of empowering individuals across all levels of an organization.

The Importance of Empowerment

Empowerment is important because it engages an individual's inherent motivation. When individuals feel empowered, they are more inclined to take initiative, think creatively, and put in extra effort. Empowerment creates a sense of ownership, allowing team members to recognize the significance of their contributions and understand that they have a role in the outcome.

Take into account Google, a company well-known for its innovative culture. A significant factor contributing to Google's success is its policy of allowing employees to dedicate "20% time" to projects of their own choosing. This policy has resulted in the development of several of Google's most successful products, such as Gmail and Google News. It is clear that empowering individuals to pursue their ideas and embrace risks can lead to truly transformative outcomes.

The Psychological Effects of Empowerment

Empowerment has a significant psychological effect. It fosters confidence, improves job satisfaction, and alleviates stress. When individuals perceive that they have authority over their tasks and are entrusted with decision-making, they are more inclined to feel a sense of fulfillment. This consequently results in increased engagement and productivity.

Studies conducted by organizational psychologists indicate that empowerment is strongly associated with beneficial results, including enhanced job performance, reduced turnover rates, and improved overall well-being. Empowerment fosters a positive cycle: when individuals feel empowered, their motivation increases, resulting in improved performance, which in turn strengthens their sense of empowerment.

Mentoring: The Art of Guiding Others

Mentoring acts as an important tool for empowerment. It entails guiding, supporting, and nurturing others' growth, often by sharing knowledge, experiences, and insights. A mentor is more than merely a teacher; they act as a coach, a trusted confidant, and a role model. Mentors create an environment in which mentees can explore their potential, take calculated risks, and learn from their experiences.

Understanding the Significance of Mentorship

A mentor's role encompasses much more than merely imparting knowledge. Active listening, comprehension, and empathy towards the mentee's experiences are essential. A mentor should demonstrate patience, open-mindedness, and a non-judgmental approach, creating an environment that allows the mentee to express themselves openly and seek clarification without fear.

Mentoring is a process of mutual exchange. The mentor provides support, and the mentee shares their unique viewpoints and experiences within the relationship. This interaction creates a meaningful learning experience for all participants, promoting growth and development.

The Mentoring Process: Establishing Trust and Rapport

Trust is the cornerstone of a successful mentoring relationship. In the absence of trust, the mentee might be reluctant to express themselves, discuss their difficulties, or ask for guidance. Establishing trust takes time, consistency, and genuine interaction. It requires a sincere investment in the mentee's development and a dedication to their success.

Building rapport is an essential component. Building a strong rapport encourages open communication, mutual respect, and a sense of camaraderie. It facilitates genuine and constructive feedback, which is crucial for the mentee's growth. Building rapport can be accomplished through consistent interactions, attentive listening, and demonstrating empathy.

Approaches for Successful Mentoring

A structured approach is essential for effective mentoring. Here are several strategies that can assist mentors in empowering their mentees:

1. Establish Clear Goals: Collaborate with the mentee to define clear and attainable objectives. The goals must be specific, measurable, and in harmony with the mentee's aspirations. A clear direction enhances the mentoring process and establishes a framework for assessing progress.

2. Promote self-reflection: Support the mentee in examining their experiences, strengths, and opportunities for growth. Self-reflection promotes self-awareness, an essential component for both personal and professional development.

3. Provide Constructive Feedback: While feedback is a valuable tool for development, it requires careful communication. Concentrate on delivering feedback that is detailed, practical, and encouraging. Refrain from excessive criticism, as it may diminish the mentee's confidence.

4. Model Behavior: As a mentor, your actions carry more weight than your words. Demonstrate the behaviors, attitudes, and values you want to impart to your mentee. This involves showcasing integrity, resilience, and a dedication to ongoing learning.

5. Acknowledge Achievements: It is important to recognize and celebrate the mentee's accomplishments, regardless of their size. Recognizing achievements enhances the mentee's self-assurance and strengthens constructive behaviors.

6. Be accessible: Ensure that you are available to the mentee through regular meetings, phone calls, or emails. Demonstrating accessibility reflects your dedication to the mentoring relationship and the mentee's growth.

Case Study: Mentorship in Practice

Take, for instance, the case of Steve Jobs and Tim Cook. Upon receiving his cancer diagnosis, Jobs started preparing Cook, who was then the COO, to take over as CEO of Apple. Jobs' mentorship extended beyond the technical aspects of the role; he also conveyed the significance of Apple's culture, vision, and values. Over the years, Jobs provided guidance that enabled Cook to assume the role with both confidence and competence. Today, Cook has effectively guided Apple to new heights, showcasing the enduring influence of strong mentoring.

Coaching: Empowering Through Action

Mentoring emphasizes guidance and development, whereas coaching is centered on action and performance. It entails assisting individuals in enhancing their skills, navigating challenges, and reaching their objectives. A coach serves as a catalyst, igniting change and fostering progress through focused interventions.

The Coaching Mindset

To be an effective coach, it is essential to embrace a mindset centered on empowerment. This involves having faith in the capabilities of others, exercising patience with their growth, and motivating them to take responsibility for their own development. A coaching mindset embodies optimism, resilience, and a dedication to ongoing development.

The Coaching Process: From Awareness to Action

The coaching process generally consists of multiple stages:

1. Awareness: The initial phase of coaching involves assisting the individual in recognizing their present circumstances, strengths, and opportunities for growth. This typically includes self-evaluation, input from peers, and thoughtful consideration.

2. Goal Setting: After establishing awareness, the subsequent step is to define clear and actionable goals. The goals must align with the individual's aspirations and should encourage growth and improvement.

3. Action Planning: After establishing goals, the coach works with the individual to develop an action plan. This plan must detail the specific steps, resources, and timelines necessary to achieve the goals.

4. Execution: The individual proceeds to take action, putting the plan into effect and striving towards their goals. The coach offers support, encouragement, and guidance during this process.

5. Review and Reflect: Following a period of action, the coach and the individual assess the progress achieved, consider what was effective and what was not, and modify the plan as necessary.

Techniques for Effective Coaching

Effective coaching involves various techniques that enable individuals to take charge of their personal development. Below are several important techniques:

1. Active Listening: Listening serves as the cornerstone of successful coaching. By listening attentively to the individual's concerns, aspirations, and challenges, the coach can gain a deeper understanding of their needs and offer more focused support.

2. Thought-Provoking Questions: Posing thought-provoking, open-ended questions prompts the individual to engage in critical thinking and consider various viewpoints. For instance, rather than inquiring, "Did you meet your goal?" you might ask, "What insights did you gain from the experience of striving towards your goal?"

3. Reframing: This process assists the individual in viewing a situation from an alternative perspective. This method can be especially effective in addressing challenges and transforming limiting beliefs. For instance, when an individual perceives a setback as a failure, the coach may reinterpret it as a significant learning opportunity.

4. Fostering Accountability: With empowerment comes the responsibility to act. As a coach, it is crucial to motivate the individual to take responsibility for their actions and hold themselves accountable for their development. This could include establishing regular check-ins or developing accountability frameworks.

Recognizing achievements and learning from mistakes are essential components of effective coaching. Recognizing achievements strengthens positive actions, and examining setbacks offers important lessons for future development.

Case Study: Coaching for Transformation

The narrative of Bill Campbell, commonly known as "The Coach of Silicon Valley," illustrates an exemplary instance of coaching. Campbell provided coaching to several of the most successful leaders in technology, such as Steve Jobs, Eric Schmidt, and Jeff Bezos. His approach was highly individualized—he concentrated not only on the professional advancement of his clients but also on their personal development. Campbell's coaching philosophy centered on empowerment; he recognized his clients' potential and facilitated its realization through encouragement, accountability, and profound trust.

Fostering a Culture of Growth and Development

Empowering others involves more than just personal interactions; it requires fostering an environment where empowerment is standard practice. This entails promoting a culture that supports ongoing learning, innovation, and teamwork. In this culture, every individual is regarded as a leader, and each person has the chance to play a role in the organization's success.

Creating a Learning Organization

A learning organization emphasizes ongoing enhancement and motivates its members to pursue new knowledge and skills. This culture promotes empowerment by providing individuals with the necessary tools and opportunities for growth.

Approaches to Nurturing a Growth-Oriented Culture

1. Foster a Culture of Continuous Learning: Support employees in their pursuit of further education, participation in workshops, and engagement in training programs. Facilitate access to resources, including online courses, books, and industry conferences. Investing in continuous learning enables your team to remain at the forefront and contribute innovative ideas.

2. Promote Experimentation: Foster a supportive atmosphere where team members feel at ease exploring new ideas, even in the face of potential failure. Foster an innovative mindset, viewing failure as a chance to learn instead of a hindrance. This method encourages creativity and enables individuals to think innovatively.

3. Facilitate Growth Opportunities: Provide opportunities for career advancement, such as promotions, leadership roles, or interdisciplinary projects. Encourage your team members to embrace new challenges and enhance their skill sets. By providing clear pathways for growth, you demonstrate your commitment to their development and allow them to take charge of their careers.

4. Encourage Collaboration: Collaboration plays a vital role in fostering empowerment. Foster collaboration among team members, promote the exchange of ideas, and nurture each other's development. Facilitate cross-functional collaboration by bringing together individuals from various departments to address challenges and foster innovation. Creating a collaborative environment enables your team to utilize one another's strengths and attain greater success together.

5. Lead by Example: As a leader, your actions establish the standard for the organization. Exemplify the behaviors and attitudes you want to cultivate within your team. Demonstrate a dedication to ongoing learning, experimentation, and teamwork. When you lead by example, you inspire others to do the same and foster a culture of growth.

Conclusion: The Impact of Empowerment

Empowering others goes beyond being a mere leadership strategy; it embodies a philosophy capable of transforming both lives and organizations. Empowering those in our vicinity generates a ripple effect that reaches well beyond our immediate community. Individuals who feel empowered naturally emerge as leaders, motivating and uplifting those around them.

This chapter has examined the principles of empowerment, the significance of mentoring and coaching, and the strategies for cultivating a culture of growth and development. By adopting these principles, you can empower those around you, fostering an environment where everyone can succeed.

As you progress in your leadership journey, keep in mind that empowerment serves as a significant catalyst for change. Empowering others not only fosters their success but also enhances your own. A genuine leader is someone who fosters the development of more leaders rather than merely accumulating followers.

Worksheet: Empowering Others

The purpose of this worksheet is to assist you in implementing the principles of empowerment, mentoring, and coaching in your personal life and leadership journey.

1. Consider a moment when you experienced a sense of empowerment

- Share an experience in which you felt a genuine sense of empowerment.

- What were the conditions surrounding this situation? Who has empowered you, and in what ways?

- How did this experience influence your confidence, motivation, and performance?

2. Recognize Opportunities to Enable Others

- Consider your existing team or network of influence. Who stands to gain from empowerment?

- What particular steps can you implement to support these individuals? Think about offering mentoring, coaching, or opportunities for development.

3. Establish Empowerment Objectives

- Establish three clear objectives for empowering others over the next three months.

- These objectives ought to be practical, quantifiable, and in harmony with the individual's requirements and ambitions.

4. Organize Your Mentoring or Coaching Sessions

- Select an individual whom you would like to mentor or coach. Develop a structured plan for your sessions, detailing objectives, frequency, and essential topics to address.

5. Evaluate Your Progress

- Take a moment to consider the advancements you've made in

supporting and uplifting others over the past three months.

- What were the successful aspects?

- What obstacles did you encounter?

- What steps can you take to enhance your approach in the future?

Action Points

Begin Empowering Today: Start by empowering an individual within your team or sphere of influence. Consider implementing gradual changes, such as giving them greater autonomy on a project or extending an offer to mentor them.

Set an example: Demonstrate empowerment through your actions. Demonstrate a dedication to ongoing learning, exploration, and teamwork.

Foster a Growth Culture: Promote a culture of growth by supporting ongoing learning, experimentation, and collaboration within your organization or community.

Reflect Regularly: Consistently take time to evaluate your initiatives aimed at empowering others. Modify your strategy as necessary to guarantee that you are successfully fostering their development.

Final Reflection

As you finish this chapter, take a moment to consider how you can incorporate the principles of empowerment into your everyday life. What steps can you take to foster growth and development in your surroundings? Empowerment goes beyond assisting others in achieving success; it involves establishing a legacy of leadership that motivates and elevates those in your vicinity.

Chapter 10

CONTINUOUS GROWTH AND DEVELOPMENT

Leadership is frequently perceived as a destination—a peak of accomplishment that, once attained, marks the conclusion of a journey. True leadership is not a fixed position; it is an evolving process, a continuous journey of growth and development. Effective leaders recognize that the quest for excellence is an ongoing journey. They welcome the notion that there is always additional knowledge to acquire, another skill to enhance, and a new challenge to tackle.

This chapter concludes our journey in discovering how to unleash your inner hero while embodying integrity, strength, and compassion in your leadership. We will explore the idea of continuous growth and development, analyzing its importance for maintaining effective leadership in the long run. We will examine effective strategies for fostering a mindset of continuous learning, highlight the significance of adaptability, and reflect on ways to maintain relevance in a constantly evolving environment.

As we enter this final chapter, keep in mind that leadership involves not resting on past achievements but continually seeking improvement. Regardless of your experience level as a leader, the principles outlined here will act as a guiding compass, steering you toward a continuous journey of learning and personal growth.

The Continuous Path of Leadership

The Illusion of Arrival

One of the most widespread misconceptions in leadership is the notion of *"arrival."* This myth implies that upon attaining a specific level of success—be it a title, a position, or a collection of achievements—you have completed your journey. In essence, leadership is not a destination; it is an ongoing journey of progress.

Reflect on the journey of Nelson Mandela, a figure who exemplified ongoing development throughout his lifetime. Despite spending 27 years in prison, Mandela did not see his release as the end of his journey. He viewed it as a new beginning, a fresh opportunity to learn, grow, and make an impact. Mandela recognized that leadership involves not just celebrating past accomplishments but also adapting and growing to face new challenges.

The notion of arrival can be perilous because it promotes a sense of complacency. Leaders who think they have "arrived" may become stagnant, losing their motivation to innovate and enhance their efforts. They may cease to seek feedback, become resistant to change, or struggle to adapt to new circumstances. Conversely, leaders who perceive their journey as continuous tend to remain curious, open-minded, and actively engaged. They recognize that leadership is a journey of development rather than a fixed state.

Adopting a Growth Mindset

The concept of a growth mindset, popularized by psychologist Carol Dweck, lies at the core of continuous development. The belief in a growth mindset is that one can cultivate their abilities and intelligence through commitment, effort, and continuous learning. A fixed mindset, on the other hand, holds the belief that our abilities are unchanging and fixed.

Leaders who possess a growth mindset tend to welcome challenges, persist through difficulties, and view effort as essential to achieving mastery. They perceive failure not as a measure of their innate capabilities but as an important opportunity for growth and learning. This perspective fosters ongoing growth as it motivates leaders to identify opportunities for development, even in challenging or uncertain circumstances.

Consider the case of Satya Nadella, the CEO of Microsoft. Nadella's growth mindset played a crucial role in revitalizing Microsoft, a technology giant that had diminished its innovative prowess when he assumed leadership in 2014. He fostered an environment of learning and experimentation, where employees felt empowered to take risks and embrace failure. This change in perspective enabled Microsoft to reclaim its status as a leader in the technology sector, showcasing the importance of ongoing development in leadership.

The Significance of Feedback and Reflection

Continuous growth necessitates a dedication to self-awareness, and one of the most effective methods to foster this is through feedback and reflection. Feedback offers leaders an external viewpoint on their actions, choices, and influence, whereas reflection enables them to internalize these insights and incorporate them into their development process.

Leaders such as Howard Schultz, the former CEO of Starbucks, have consistently acknowledged the importance of feedback. Schultz encouraged employees at every level to share honest feedback, fostering an environment where constructive criticism was appreciated and embraced.

The open culture of feedback at Starbucks has enabled the company to remain agile and responsive to both internal and external changes, which has played a significant role in its sustained success.

Nonetheless, feedback by itself is insufficient. Leaders should regularly evaluate their experiences, learning, evolution, and areas for improvement. Reflection enables leaders to link their experiences with their growth, transforming feedback into practical insights.

One effective method to integrate reflection into your leadership practice is by utilizing journaling. Regularly documenting your thoughts, challenges, and learnings allows you to monitor your progress, recognize patterns, and make better-informed decisions regarding your development. This straightforward yet impactful tool can serve as a catalyst for ongoing development, assisting you in maintaining alignment with your leadership objectives.

Cultivating Adaptability in Leadership

The Importance of Being Adaptable

In a world that is ever-evolving, adaptability is an essential skill for leaders rather than merely a desirable trait. Leaders must be flexible, resilient, and open to change in response to the rapid pace of technological advancement, shifting economic landscapes, and evolving societal expectations.

Examine the situation at Kodak, which was once a leading force in the photography industry. Kodak's decline is frequently linked to its inability to adjust to the digital revolution. Kodak was one of the pioneers in digital camera technology; however, it held onto its film-based business model for an extended period, which ultimately contributed to its decline. This example underscores the risks associated with inflexibility and emphasizes the vital role of adaptability in leadership.

Leaders who demonstrate adaptability are more capable of managing uncertainty, addressing unforeseen challenges, and capitalizing on emerging opportunities. They demonstrate a willingness to pivot, reassess their strategies, and welcome change. Adaptability enables leaders to remain relevant and effective in a changing environment, ensuring their organizations can prosper even amidst disruption.

Approaches to Enhance Adaptability

Developing adaptability starts with fostering a mindset that embraces change. This entails releasing strict thinking patterns and adopting a more adaptable and flexible method for problem-solving and decision-making. Here are several strategies to improve adaptability in leadership:

1. Stay Informed: Remain updated on industry trends, technological advancements, and societal changes. Being well-informed enables you to foresee changes and modify your strategies as needed. Leaders who understand their environment's larger context are better equipped to adapt and succeed.

2. Promote Innovation: Cultivate an environment that supports innovative thinking within your organization. Motivate your team to explore innovative ideas, embrace thoughtful risks, and gain insights from setbacks. Innovation frequently results in fresh solutions and opportunities, enabling your organization to maintain a competitive edge.

3. Cultivate Emotional Intelligence: Adaptability is closely related to emotional intelligence, which entails understanding and managing your own emotions as well as those of others. Leaders who possess strong emotional intelligence are more adept at managing change, as they can effectively navigate the emotional intricacies that frequently arise during such transitions.

4. Practice Agility: Agility refers to the capacity to respond swiftly and effortlessly to changes. Establishing systems and processes that facilitate quick decision-making and implementation can foster this development. Agile leaders can quickly adjust their strategies, helping their organizations stay competitive in a rapidly changing environment.

5. Foster a Culture of Learning: Promote ongoing education and development within your organization. A team that is dedicated to learning is better equipped to adapt to new challenges and seize opportunities. Leaders should exemplify a commitment to their own growth and development, setting a standard for a learning culture throughout the organization.

The Importance of Resilience

Adaptability and resilience are closely interconnected. Resilience is the ability to quickly bounce back from challenges while maintaining focus and determination when faced with difficulties. Resilience is essential in leadership to maintain adaptability over the long term.

Resilient leaders remain undeterred by setbacks or obstacles. They see these as opportunities for learning and growth. They uphold an optimistic perspective, even in challenging situations, and motivate their teams to adopt a similar attitude. Resilience allows leaders to maintain their direction, adjust to evolving circumstances, and ultimately reach their objectives.

The story of Jeff Bezos and Amazon serves as a notable example of resilience in leadership. During its initial phase, Amazon encountered various obstacles, such as doubt from investors and intense rivalry. Bezos's resilience and adaptability enabled him to navigate the challenges faced by the company, ultimately transforming Amazon into one of the most successful enterprises globally.

Maintaining Relevance in a Dynamic Environment

The Importance of Staying Relevant

In the fast-paced environment of today, maintaining relevance is a significant challenge for leaders. The skills, knowledge, and strategies that led to success in the past may not suffice to maintain it in the future. Leaders must consistently enhance their skills, expand their knowledge, and adjust their strategies to address the changing needs of their industry and society in order to remain effective.

Leadership relevance extends beyond merely keeping up with trends; it involves grasping the wider context of your leadership role and having the ability to foresee and adapt to changes. Leaders who maintain their relevance are proactive, forward-thinking, and highly aware of the needs of their organizations and the surrounding world.

Lifelong Learning as a Means to Stay Relevant

Lifelong learning is essential for maintaining relevance. In a time when information is always changing, leaders need to dedicate themselves to ongoing education—be it through formal studies, self-guided learning, or hands-on experiences.

1. Formal Education:

Participating in leadership development programs, attending workshops, or pursuing advanced degrees can offer leaders fresh perspectives, valuable tools, and effective frameworks to improve their capabilities. Formal education provides a systematic approach to enhance your knowledge and skills, ensuring you remain at the leading edge of your profession.

2. Independent Learning:

Self-directed learning means assuming responsibility for your own educational journey. This may involve engaging with books, tuning into podcasts, or keeping up with influential figures in your field. By actively pursuing new information, you can remain updated on the latest trends and developments.

3. Experiential Learning:

Experiential learning involves acquiring knowledge and skills through practical experience. It requires leaving your comfort zone, embracing new challenges, and contemplating your experiences. This form of learning is especially effective as it enables the application of theoretical knowledge in practical scenarios, enhancing your comprehension and refining your abilities.

The Influence of Networks and Mentorship

Remaining relevant necessitates the development and upkeep of robust networks. Your network serves as a significant resource for information, support, and inspiration. Connecting with other leaders, industry experts, and peers allows you to gain insights into emerging trends, share best practices, and learn from the experiences of others.

Mentorship serves as an effective means of maintaining relevance. A mentor can offer valuable guidance, share their experiences, and provide a new perspective on your leadership journey. Engaging in mentoring relationships, whether as a mentor or a mentee, can be profoundly rewarding, providing valuable opportunities for personal and professional growth.

Adapting to Technological Change

Technology is one of the most significant drivers of change in today's world. Technological advancements, including artificial intelligence, blockchain, and virtual reality, are transforming industries and altering the skill sets required for leaders to thrive. To remain relevant, leaders must not only stay informed about these changes but also comprehend how to utilize them to their benefit.

Leaders such as Elon Musk have shown the significance of adopting technology. Musk's ventures, including Tesla and SpaceX, represent the forefront of innovation, fueled by his profound understanding of and dedication to technology. By keeping pace with technological trends, Musk has successfully positioned his companies at the forefront of their industries.

The Importance of Purpose and Values

Ultimately, maintaining relevance as a leader necessitates remaining aligned with your purpose and values. In a world that is ever-evolving, your purpose and values can provide a reliable foundation, steering your decisions and actions. Leaders who understand their purpose and values are more adept at managing change, as they possess a strong sense of direction and a clear set of guiding principles.

Leaders such as Malala Yousafzai exemplify the strength of purposeful leadership. Yousafzai has consistently demonstrated her unwavering dedication to promoting girls' education, even in the face of significant challenges. Her strong sense of purpose has not only kept her relevant but has also inspired millions globally.

Actionable Steps for Continuous Growth

As we wrap up this chapter, it is important to offer you practical steps that you can implement to further your journey of growth and development. Here are some effective strategies to support your journey of ongoing leadership development:

1. Define Learning Objectives: Set clear and specific learning and development goals. Mastering a new skill, deepening your knowledge in a specific area, or expanding your network can all be achieved more effectively with clear goals, which will help you maintain focus and motivation.

2. Create a Personal Development Plan: Formulate a plan that details your learning objectives, the resources required, and the steps you will undertake to reach your goals. This plan ought to be adaptable, enabling you to make adjustments as you move forward.

3. Regularly Seek Feedback: Develop a routine of obtaining feedback from peers, mentors, and team members. Use this feedback to identify areas for improvement and monitor your progress.

4. Invest in Formal Education: Think about enrolling in leadership courses, attending workshops, or pursuing advanced degrees. Formal education offers valuable tools and frameworks that can significantly improve your leadership abilities.

5. Participate in self-directed learning: Allocate time for self-directed learning. Explore literature, engage with podcasts, or keep up with influential figures in your field. Maintain a sense of curiosity and take initiative in exploring new information.

6. Foster a Growth Mindset: Welcome challenges, persist through difficulties, and recognize effort as the route to mastery. Fostering a growth mindset will enhance your resilience and adaptability.

7. Engage in reflection: Consistently take time to consider your experiences, challenges, and achievements. Engage in journaling or similar reflective practices to uncover insights about your development and pinpoint areas that may need enhancement.

8. Establish a robust network: Engage with fellow leaders, industry experts, and colleagues. Leverage your network for valuable insights, assistance, and motivation.

9. Embrace Technology: Keep yourself updated on technological trends and think about how you can utilize them to improve your leadership effectiveness.

10. Lead with intention: Remain committed to your purpose and core values. Utilize them as a framework to steer through change and make choices that are in harmony with your long-term vision.

Conclusion

Leadership is a journey rather than a destination—an ongoing commitment to growth, development, and excellence. As we reach the end of this book, keep in mind that the principles we have explored are not fixed; they are intended to grow alongside you as you advance in your leadership journey.

Ongoing growth and development are essential for maintaining effective leadership over time. Embracing a growth mindset, remaining adaptable, and dedicating yourself to lifelong learning will help you stay a relevant and impactful leader in a constantly evolving world. As you progress, continue to pursue new opportunities for learning, growth, and making a positive impact. Your path as a leader is just starting to unfold.

This chapter serves as a reminder that the most successful leaders are those who continually pursue growth. They recognize that leadership is defined not by past experiences but by future direction. As you step into a leadership role, continue to strive for improvement, maintain your curiosity, and welcome the challenges that arise. By taking this step, you will not only reveal your inner hero but also motivate others to follow suit.

Your Feedback is Important!

Thank You for Reading!

Dear Reader,

Thank you for taking the time to read my work. Sharing resourceful information and ideas with readers like you is one of the greatest joys of being an author.

If you found this book valuable, entertaining, or thought-provoking—or even if you have suggestions for improvement—I'd greatly appreciate your honest feedback in a review. Your thoughts not only help me grow but also guide other readers in discovering books they might enjoy or find useful.

Leaving a review is simple, and it makes a big difference. Thank you for your support—it truly means a lot!

With gratitude!

Eden Nora

ABOUT THE AUTHOR

Paul Sam is a distinguished author and thought leader in the realm of Relationship & Dating, Self-Help. With an insightful blend of professional expertise and personal experience, Paul has dedicated his career to empowering individuals to cultivate meaningful relationships and personal growth. His work is celebrated for its depth, clarity, and transformative impact, making him a revered figure in the self-help community.

Paul holds advanced degrees in Psychology and Human Behavior, equipping him with a profound understanding of the complexities of human relationships. His academic background is complemented by certifications in life coaching and relationship counseling, ensuring a well-rounded approach to his work. Paul's career spans over two decades, during which he has conducted extensive research and led workshops that have touched the lives of thousands.

Drawing from his own life experiences, Paul brings authenticity and relatability to his writing. Having navigated the challenges of maintaining lasting relationships in a fast-paced modern world, he offers practical advice rooted in real-world scenarios. His personal journey of self-discovery and growth is woven into his narratives, providing readers with a genuine and empathetic perspective.

Paul's books and seminars resonate deeply with a diverse audience that includes young professionals, couples, and individuals seeking personal development. His ability to connect with readers across different demographics is a testament to his keen market awareness and his commitment to addressing the unique needs and aspirations of his audience. Through meticulous market research and qualitative analysis, Paul crafts content that is not only relevant but also profoundly impactful.

Paul's bestselling books are been translated into multiple languages, in order to reach a global audience eager for guidance in the delicate art of relationship building. As a frequent speaker at international conferences and a regular contributor to leading self-help publications, Paul continues to shape the conversation around personal and relational well-being. His articulate and engaging communication style has made him a sought-after guest on various media platforms.

Paul Sam's unwavering dedication to his readers is evident in the thoughtful and actionable insights he provides. His authoritative yet approachable tone invites readers to embark on a journey of self-improvement and relational fulfillment. By following Paul's work, readers gain access to a wealth of knowledge and inspiration that promises to enrich their lives and relationships.

In a world where genuine connection is more essential than ever, Paul Sam stands as a beacon of wisdom and guidance. His work not only informs but also inspires, offering a pathway to deeper understanding and meaningful change.

ALSO BY PAUL SAM

1. Revitalize Your Marriage: 7 Proven Steps to Better Communication and Connection

2. Finding Happiness Together: 10 Steps to a Conflict-Free, Independent, and Joyful Marriage

3. Unmasking Deceit: A Practical Guide to Spotting Manipulative Behaviors

4. Rise to Lead: A Guide to Unleashing Your Inner Hero and Stop Being Taken Advantage Of

5. The Attraction Advantage: Your Guide to Attracting Attention, Finding Love and Winning His Heart

6. The Magic of Positive Affirmation: The Magic of Positive Affirmation: Transforming Limiting Beliefs into Limitless Possibilities Through Positive Self-Talk